The Last Stork Summer

t Stor
 mes

j d salinger

The Last Stork Summer

Mary Brigid Surber

**TOP HAT
BOOKS**

Winchester, UK
Washington, USA

First published by Top Hat Books, 2015
Top Hat Books is an imprint of John Hunt Publishing Ltd., Laurel House, Station Approach,
Alresford, Hants, SO24 9JH, UK
office1@jhpbooks.net
www.johnhuntpublishing.com

For distributor details and how to order please visit the 'Ordering' section on our website.

Text copyright: Mary Brigid Surber 2014

ISBN: 978 1 78279 934 4
Library of Congress Control Number: 2014954145

A CIP catalogue record for this book is available from the British Library.

Design: Stuart Davies

Printed and bound by CPI Group (UK) Ltd, Croydon, CR0 4YY, UK

We operate a distinctive and ethical publishing philosophy in all
areas of our business, from our global network of authors to
production and worldwide distribution.

This is not my story, but it was given to me to tell,
so I will tell it.
I may not be the best teller, but I will tell it the best I can.

In west-central Poland, near the German border where two brooks converge, a vast wetland is formed. Along the River Warta, just upstream from the marsh, sits my town. Legend has it that as the city was built, the founding fathers didn't know what to name it. Someone suggested that the city council sit outside the town gate and take the name of the person who entered first. The older men went outside the walls to wait; soon a young girl came. Upon entering, the council asked her for her name.

She said, "I'm Kusters Trin." So the city was named Kustrin; in Poland we called it Kostrzyn.

My name is Eva. In Polish, it is spelled Ewa. My name means "life."

As an only child, I loved the land where I was born and lived my earliest memories. I couldn't imagine growing up anywhere else. In my mind's eye I can still see the green of the watery lowlands that stretched beyond our land, the blue of the sky, and the white of the storks. They came in spring and left at the end of the harvesting. This caused me great regret because I knew their leaving meant the summer's end and school's beginning. The sky seemed so blue that summer; the summer before the war changed everything about the land and life that I loved; the summer of freedom when I last laid eyes on the green of the wetlands, the blue of the sky, and the white of the storks.

The summer I call the last stork summer.

Chapter 1

Creation

The scientific name of the European White stork is: *Ciconia ciconia.*

Creation: usually associated with making life. Poland was overflowing with potential and the abundance of life...creation.

Grandpa said, "If God came down from heaven, He'd come to Poland because it would remind Him of the Garden of Eden."

I wondered why God would ever want to come here, especially with the infiniteness of the universe. It wasn't that I doubted my grandfather's words or Poland's potential. It was mankind's wars over boundaries, causing problems in the world that made me question grandpa's statement. Over the centuries our country had been torn apart by countless wars and struggles for land. We lived and worked on a farm that had been in my mother's family for a very long time. Land that meant more than just a place to live and work. Land that we nurtured, coaxed to life, exchanged favors with. Living here gave me lots of opportunity to see life's potential. Hitler must have seen it too.

Nine days before Germany invaded Poland, Adolf Hitler commanded his military officers to: "kill without pity or mercy, all men, women, and children of Polish descent or language. Only in this way can we obtain the living space [*lebensraum*] we need." And so, the terrorizing of the Polish people began on September 1, 1939. By creating his world he was destroying ours.

* * *

It was a beautiful summer morning. The light came in chunks of vividness, making the world around me richer and more distinct.

It was the kind of sunrise that makes you want to linger by the window so your eyes can take in creation awakening, unfolding before you, but I was not allowed to remain a spectator to daybreak, or to leave the house that day. I found my family huddled around the radio in the kitchen, clinging to a hope that would never be realized. They were listening to the words flying out of the box, like geese in formation, one following the other making their imprint on the pages of my brain. Their concentration floated over the radio like a bird hovering in the wind. It remained unbroken by the words of shock and distress exposing Poland's vulnerability.

In the distance, I could hear squadrons of planes, charting their way toward the east, making clear blue skies turn black and gray. Metal birds carrying bombs and dropping destruction, changing the topography of the land and the life of its people. Eventually, the noise of the war drove us to the root cellar just outside our kitchen.

Down the steps into the cool darkness, we sat with bins of onions, potatoes, and other vegetables. I wasn't fond of this cellar before the war; dark as a moonless night, it reminded me of a grave and obscured my view of the landscape outside. Now, however, it felt completely different. It took away most of the noise of the war, and kept me feeling protected and encircled by the love and strength of my family.

After the first week of war, papa built wooden benches to sit on and mama added blankets to the stocked shelves. We were surrounded by food and sturdy earthen walls. It muffled the sound of Germany's crushing invasion taking our countryside, leaving a path of desolation in its churned up wake. Every morning began in this way, followed by days, then weeks of staying inside. I began to feel safer in the cellar than I did in the house. Here we sat, day after day, unable to witness the changes happening in eastern Poland. Kostrzyn had been taken without much of a fight. It was small, and didn't hold much importance for the Nazis; many Germans had already made this land their home. Proclamations would be made. New laws would be enforced. Poland would fall.

For a short time every morning, the radio was our only connection to the world. A world that was broken, and so different from the one I'd been born into. I looked around the cellar, desperate for a picture to place in my head, where I could keep it safely cloaked until I needed it. I searched my papa's face, willing my eyes to commit every line, every detail to memory. I studied the heaviness of his coal colored hair, the clear green eyes that saw beyond the obvious, and the sand colored flesh warmed by hours and hours of living and working on land that was part of his very being.

He saw me staring and held out his hands. I crumbled into the safety of his arms. Beneath the earth, in a cool, dark, stone-lined cellar, the days marched on; I learned the meaning of the word comfort, and that authentic strength was simply displayed in gentleness.

Kindliness could not be extended to our animals, however. We could only venture outside under cover of darkness to feed and tend to their needs. They must have missed the people who cared for them. I had no idea I'd miss the entire autumn that year. I loved the fall. Everything around me turned gold; the grain fields, meadow grass, leaves, fruit. The war kept me from seeing it, though, and I was starting to lose patience with the new routine that had been forced on us. I longed to look out across the valley and watch the seasons dress the landscape in her new colors. There was a stork nest down the hill on the roof of an abandoned barn, just beyond the edge of our farm. I knew the habits and routines of the storks that nested there. I knew it because it was real, true and certain. I knew it because I watched it every year. It wasn't something that happened occasionally; it occurred consistently, generation after generation. This year I wondered if they'd left early for their wintering grounds because of the war. Did they sense the difference in our world, or did they continue following the natural cycles of life they were accustomed to despite the challenge to Poland's survival?

Hitler's plan for Poland's destruction was thorough and carried out systematically. By the middle of October, 1939, all of our rights had vanished, and we were fully and completely under German rule and occupation. We were under strict rationing. Only bare necessities of food, fuel and medicine could be purchased. We were also subject to special legislation. This allowed Germany to forcibly draft all of our young men into the German army; they forbid us speaking the Polish language, disposed of the Polish press, and shattered our bookshops, libraries, art and culture. All secondary schools and colleges were closed and all churches and synagogues were burned. Street signs as well as cities were renamed in German. Most of the priests as well as any community leaders, teachers, judges, doctors, and mayors, were publicly shot or sent to concentration camps.

Polish nationalism and Catholicism had been inseparable for years. The Catholic Church provided the foundation for Polish nationalism by rejecting Hitler's theories and practices of racial purification, and preaching unity of the human race. Organizationally, the Church offered networks and institutions within which people could gather, distance themselves from Nazi propaganda, provide aid to Nazi victims, and oppose Nazi policies. In certain occupied regions, Catholic resistance was "armed." If the Nazis were to succeed they had to destroy the church organization as well as its leadership. The first clergymen to arrive in concentration camps were the Polish priests. Along with the clergy, Poland's educated class was specifically targeted. Hitler knew that controlling the country would be much easier without them.

By the end of December 1939, the "street round-ups" started. These continued for the duration of the war. People were forcibly taken from their homes in the middle of the night. Those living in cities were the first to experience the terror, confusion and helplessness of the round-ups. After being forced at gunpoint from their homes, Polish citizens were lined up for hours, with no regard for their need of food, water, or shelter. They were interrogated and their fates sealed. Those chosen for deportation were categorized by their occupational status, or the attitude they maintained toward the Germans. A few would be allowed to return to their home; most, however, were either sent to work camps, concentration camps, or immediately shot...dismissed, depreciated, and discarded.

By the spring of 1941, the Polish children became the next target of the German war machine. The children with "Aryan Characteristics" were taken from their families and sent to Lodz, in eastern Poland, for further examinations. Children who passed the examinations were placed with German families or in German orphanages to continue their cultural re-education. Children who didn't pass the examinations and children who didn't qualify were sent to labor camps to begin a life of confinement and deprivation. By December of 1942 a special camp for Polish children was established within a separate area of the Lodz ghetto.

* * *

I would lie in bed at night and listen to my parents and grand-parents discuss our situation.

"We are not in a city, nor near one. We live near a small town, but unfortunately we are also close to what used to be the German border," said papa. "We have managed to survive this way for three years, our luck will hold," he added with tired resignation.

"We can hide in the woods," offered mama. "Many of the families from this area are doing that."

"Yes, but you know what happens to them if they are discovered…" Papa left the sentence unfinished. There was no need to finish it. We all knew the price.

"I can't sit here any longer and wait for them to come and take Ewa," said mama. "There must be a way to keep her safe."

I could hear the panic in my mother's voice and feel the helplessness she felt. She carried her regret like a sack of grain strapped to her back. Remaining on our land while hoping for immunity from Nazi policies, was like hoping to survive a burning house by staying inside. I knew it was more than she could bear. I could see the sadness in her eyes and feel the despair in her heart. Surrounded by destruction and chaos it was almost impossible not to feel that way. Over the past three years we had watched helplessly as Germany dismantled our country, culture, and lives.

Other than one old cow, a few chickens and two sheep, all of our farm animals had been taken. Only the land immediately surrounding the house was still ours. The rest of our farm had been given to a German family. Everything we'd known was gone; vanished, like it had never existed. Other families in the area had simply disappeared, gone into hiding, or been deported by the Nazis to labor camps. There seemed to be no way out. Our time was running out and we were painfully aware of it. Like watching leaves change color, then floating away in the winter wind, we were watching the substance of our lives transform and disappear. The first three years of the war showed me that only the seasons, and the storks following their yearly migration and nesting routines, remained constant in Poland. Everything else was changed by Hitler. It didn't feel real. It didn't feel possible, but it was.

I will never forget my last morning at home. After waking and dressing, I walked into the kitchen. A heavy sadness hung in the air. Basil stood next to me, resting his head on my leg as I rubbed his ear. My mother and grandmother were seated at the table; my grandmother was holding my mother's hand. Eyes swollen from crying, my mother's face bore the heart-break of our dilemma. I had never seen such a sad look in my mother's eyes.

"It's ok, mama," I offered. I couldn't bear seeing her so sad. No one had to tell me. I knew my summons had been delivered. My appearance was expected at the deportation center in Kostrzyn. My day for racial examination had arrived.

Chapter 2

Sovereignty

Storks migrate back and forth from their wintering grounds in Africa to their spring and summer range in Poland.

They are attracted to tall trees or buildings where they build nests that often weigh several tons.

There was a family living on a farm, near a marsh along the River Warta. The day after Ewa left, mama awoke to find her husband lying next to her, staring at the ceiling. A single tear ran down his cheek.

"Is it true?" she whispered.

Papa shook his head to confirm the heaviness that was taking over her chest and making it difficult to breathe. Hair wild, eyes the color of inconsolable grief, she rocked back and forth screaming silently. She begged God to end the nightmare. Basil, who'd been sleeping on the floor next to their bed, slowly climbed up and placed his head on her chest for a few moments, then stood and howled, making the most sorrowful sound she'd ever heard an animal make. His wail bore witness to her silent screams and gave sound to the grief she could not voice.

* * *

Sovereignty is authority claimed by a community. We were now firmly controlled by Nazi authority. We were part of all the lands, people, and resources that Adolf Hitler claimed for Germany. How could a mad-man named Adolf Hitler incite the German people to wage war on their neighbors, kidnap close to 200,000 Polish children, and enslave them in labor camps?

In March 1942, I arrived at the work camp within the walls of the Lodz ghetto. At first it was the lack of green that made me cringe. No nature, just bare russet boxes, laid out in rows, surrounded by miles and miles of barbed wire. They reminded me of weathered bales of hay, abandoned, and left to rot in the fields. There was only dirt, and brown, and depletion. The significance of Litzmannstadt was told by the barren, plank walls, and the rows of bunks cradling sleeping, rag-clad, misery. This was a place where hope died upon entering, but memories multiplied and sustained those fortunate enough to have them. I learned quickly to recall with vivid detail, all the little things that made life before the war so special. That was how I remembered who I was before I became a number and a non-member of Hitler's Aryan society. The memory of my mother's hugs with her long hair tickling my face was one of the first clear pictures I saw in my mind, shortly after my arrival.

I was standing in the shower room, soaking wet, naked, goose-bumps invading my normally smooth skin, shivering from fear as well as cold. I watched my long, dark brown hair fall in clumps on the floor. We were lined up after our shower, waiting and watching helplessly as we each lost our hair. The cutters were just dull scissors, and they left lumpy, unevenly spaced, short clumps of hair all over our heads. I lifted my hand in astonishment to feel my head. I'd never been without hair before. Bumpy, poking bits of fiber replaced what my head had previously worn. I thought of our sheep at shearing time. Knees knocking, heart racing, gasping the terrified air around me, I shut my eyes. That's when memories of my mother came to me, and helped relieve the craziness engulfing me.

Suddenly, instead of feeling panicked and taking short, choppy breaths, I could breathe deeply. I didn't want to see this room anymore, or feel the coldness of its purpose. I still felt shaky and scared, but the picture in my mind helped calm me.

Then the girl behind me started sobbing when her thick, curly hair hit the floor. I closed my eyes again, and willed my papa's picture to appear. The guard, as large as a tank, wearing a gray wool uniform, dashed over and started yelling at her. When that didn't stop her cries, he rotated the rifle that was strapped to his chest out of the way, and pummeled her with his fists. She crashed to the floor while the beating continued, blood spraying from her mouth and nose.

The children in the room froze. They stared in disbelief, mouths hung open in shock. They tried not to watch, but were unable to escape the sound and action of what was happening in front of them. Shouts and kicks and blood tangled with arms and legs and tears, as hatred left its signature on her body, assaulting her into submission. I stared in horror at the brutal scene before me, unable to avert my eyes. Panic, the color of red, drenched my brain and clogged my ears, forcing me to shut my eyes again. I saw myself wrapped in my papa's gentle embrace. The red slowly changed to orange, then yellow and finally white, giving me the feeling that I was basking in the safety of his strength. This memory kept me from running out of the room, and from possibly receiving a beating myself. And countless scenes like that reoccurred as the war progressed and my time in Litzmannstadt continued.

In my mind, I tried to imagine how the Nazis became so mean. I pictured a schoolyard in Germany. Adolf Hitler was the absolute ruler of the playground. The recess bell rang; the uniformed pupils goose-stepped out of their classrooms, but they didn't play. Under the watchful eye of The Führer, the yard filled with children who began fighting, bullying one another, hitting, scratching, kicking and screaming. The sign hanging on the fence near the playground said, "No Playing Allowed…fight, fight, fight." The fighting continued until the bell rang signaling the end of the free for all. Those left standing lined up and marched back in. Maybe by the time they became soldiers, I reasoned, they were already experts at wounding children.

* * *

I woke early and sat on my bunk, my back against the rough, timbered wall. Usually, I was so tired I slept as long as I could, but today for some reason I wanted to take advantage of the quiet time and recall my last spring at home. What had I been doing that spring? Were my memories starting to fade? Recollections could be so comforting. In the pre-dawn light of this day, I wanted to know one thing….*when.* When would this war be over? When could I go home? When would I be held, and hugged, and pummeled by my family's love? It was the beginning of my last spring in this camp, but I didn't know that yet. I'm sure there must have been coughing or moaning coming from the broken bodies around me, but I could no longer hear them. Even the gnawing emptiness in my stomach couldn't keep me from feeling that something was changing.

Time seemed to be passing too sluggishly, like a movie running in slow motion. I had the feeling that it had to be late March or early April. The glass on the tiny, single, window of our barracks had a thin layer of frost on it and I could barely see the beginning of light on the distant horizon. The sun peeked out, unsure if she was ready to rise or not. I could feel the earth awakening from its winter's rest. I could detect it in the air, like the scent of a freshly plowed field. The dirt was saying, "I'm ready to work, come run your fingers through me, fill me with the seed you need for food," so willing to transfer its contents into nourishment and life. The trees beyond the camp had tiny green buds forming on their bare branches, making them look like they were coated in a light green fuzz.

I looked down at my work-calloused hands. I had strong hands, just like my grandma's. Early spring was when she planted our garden. She taught me how to prepare the soil by shoveling in dried manure that had been mixed with old straw used for animal bedding. She always made me get my hands in the dirt and feel the texture of the soil as well as its temperature. She could tell from the feel of the dirt if it was ready for planting or needed more work. When she worked it enough and it felt just right, she would smell it, urging me to do the same.

"Smell it, Ewa; that is the way it should smell."

Grandma knew about the land. She could tell by watching the trees surrounding our farm when it was time to prepare the soil for the garden. Just the thought of her made me feel hopeful and calm. I missed her hugs and the faint scent of lilac and roses that hung on her clothes in the spring. I knew, for me, those two smells would forever be linked with my grandmother. Sometimes, when I was out working on a farm and caught that scent in the air, I would look up expecting to see my grandmother. That smell always uncovered the expectation of seeing her along with the painful realization of my reality.

Like a beautiful song played on the piano, flowing in rhythm to create its music, the land around me was moving through seasons and cycles of life. It reminded me that life was possible. Its grace was breathtaking, creating a rhythm and music of its own, especially in the early morning light when only nature's sounds could be heard, uninterrupted by the noise of a children's labor camp and a war.

Soon the sirens would start, signaling the beginning of our day to day drudgery. Marching feet would transport the young slaves to and from the worksites–factories, farms, warehouses of misery. Then enforced routines and expectations would take over the tired bodies in an attempt to support Germany's superiority.

How many Aprils had I been here? Two or three? Like different colors of wool yarn in a sweater, they were woven together, making it difficult for me to separate them. I wondered if I'd ever be able to move through my life again, as I had before the war, the way the earth rotated year after year. I wondered if my body could survive much longer in these harsh, inhumane, conditions. I was so dirty that I considered the possibility of the earth trying to claim me back to itself before I died and returned there naturally. I was thinner than I'd ever been; I could feel my sunken stomach at night when I laid down, and my clothes felt like huge oversized drapes, but I felt strong most of the time. I realized that the emptiness that existed in my stomach didn't reside in my heart. I was still able to feel excited about the coming spring, and the possibilities of what that would bring...the end of winter, the warmth of the sun, looking for the storks, working outside, and most importantly–the possibility of the end of war.

I yearned for the warmth of the sun on my face, and the gentle, forest-scented breezes of spring to float over me, mock jasmine adding sweetness to the mix. I imagined the rain softly washing away all the dirt and sadness that covered me, but hadn't yet consumed me. I hated this place when I first saw it, with its high walls, stark, colorless buildings, and rows and rows of wire fencing. It was so foreign to anything I'd ever known before. The complete opposite of the beautiful countryside I'd grown up in. I shivered at the memory of my first view of Litzmannstadt.

* * *

I had arrived here exhausted from the long train ride with little food, and no fresh air or water. We weren't transported in train cars with comfortable seats. Instead, like a canning jar chock full of pickles, we were packed into livestock cars, carriages of death moving families from life to extinction. There were no windows; our legs grew numb from standing for hours that melted into days; confusion and fear twisted our faces into impressions of our former selves. The moaning and discomfort of fellow passengers pushed in on me, making my breathing labored. Being unable to offer help made me search my brain desperately for some kind of explanation, but there wasn't one...I was witnessing the humiliation of my fellow countrymen.

I longed for someone to make eye contact with me and acknowledge it was really as bad as it felt; to bear witness to the annihilation of the Polish people and the insanity of war. Could no one stop the immense suffering that had been forced upon us by the greed of the Nazis? We had one bucket of water a day to share with everyone in the car...and we had one bucket to use as a toilet. Many people didn't survive the transport trains. Sometimes, during the past few years, I couldn't help think that they might have been the lucky ones.

Chapter 3

Memories

Stork nests are huge: some old nests may be over six feet in diameter and nine feet in depth.

Numb from all the violence I'd witnessed, and consumed with sadness and yearning for my family, home, and dog, I didn't think I'd survive a week. I was down to one minute. *Focus on this minute. Get through this minute. Breathe, follow directions, and don't think too much.* Time is funny that way. When you want it to last, it speeds along in a race it can't bear to lose, making you call out, "Slow down, what's the hurry?" When you want it to glide like storks on an airstream, it meanders, barely moving, making you wonder if it's gone to sleep. The nights ran and the days meandered....sleep, work, work, work, sleep, work, work, work, sleep.

Slowly, as if wading through a river of remembrance, I started recalling moments from my life. Moments I'd been forced to leave behind. At first, my memories turned to longing, filling me with a profound sense of loss. A hole so big and deep I feared I would tailspin endlessly if I let myself acknowledge it. Then gradually over many days, as I allowed a few more of my memories to seep in; they sustained me and the misery changed. Just as spring changes trees from bare branches to leaves and flowers, my memories changed from what I'd left behind to what I'd return to at the end of this chaos. I learned to visit memories for comfort and strength. Each new situation that assaulted my senses would bring a fresh reflection, something to cling to, like an enormous boulder that stubbornly adheres to the side of a cliff. I only needed to hang on. Whenever I felt the vast hole of hopelessness starting to overtake me, I looked around for something to jog my thoughts, and keep me connected to my life before the war. The sounds and sights of nature were reminders of my previous life. I listened attentively to nature's subtle sounds....frogs croaking at night, flies and bees buzzing during the day, birds chirping at dawn, wind blowing through trees, even dogs barking in the evening, "talking" to each other. Nature was all around me. I needed only to observe it.

Closing my eyes, I took a long, deep breath and smelled the wood on the walls. As I did so, I remembered the storks and reflected on the many hours I'd spent observing them. I listened intently. I wanted to hear the muted sound of the storks' wings gliding overhead. The summer before the war was the last stork summer, a summer of freedom and happiness I thought about all the time. How many days had I spent that spring and summer searching for the storks, observing their habits?

The meadow with its vivid green grass had a creek running through it, slowly and calmly gurgling its way to the marsh. My shoes were wet most of the time even though I tried to keep them dry by jumping from clump to clump of green while chasing frogs. Brown frogs, golden eyes, an important food source for the storks. I enjoyed catching them and marveled at their delicate fingers and metallic eyes. Before releasing the croakers I warned them, "The storks will be back soon and you will be on the menu." They disappeared into the tall grass with a quick vault.

With Basil following at my heels, I ran down the narrow path that crisscrossed our farm. I reached the end of the path and easily jumped up on the old, weathered-wood gate. It gently rocked back and forth underneath my weight, its rusty hinges creaked like my grandmother's wooden rocking chair. Basil put his front paws up on the top board. Mouth open, tongue out, his eyes searched the horizon with me. He knew what I was looking for. I rubbed his ear as we watched. Just outside our fence a far-reaching marsh unfolded. I was eager to see the first stork this spring. They nested on the edge of town in huge nests that sat on the tops of buildings, or large trees that bordered the marsh. They hunted for food in the marsh, sustaining their life with a nice variety of small creatures. Grandpa said that whoever spotted the first stork of spring received an extra measure of luck.

Every March and April for as long as anyone could remember, the storks came. Towns and villages all over Poland welcomed their arrival, viewing them as a sign of fertility and prosperity. They are mute, making no birdcalls, but they do clatter their bills when greeting a mate, and their long heavy wings gliding through the air create an elongated swishing sound.

Grandpa always promised, "The storks are a blessing because they teach us to have faith. They bring us prosperity."

Even before I grew to fully understand the meaning of his statement, I felt the storks were special. My mind flooded with so many questions about them. How long had they been coming here? How could something that big glide so gracefully? Why do some storks have such brightly colored beaks? Why are they mute? Why do they leave at the end of summer? How did they learn to do their mating dance? How many miles do they travel in the air on their way back to Poland? Where do they rest on their long migration?

Basil stood beside me, eyes and ears alert. He knew better than to bark. He'd been my loyal companion for the past two years since I was ten. My father, against his better judgment, presented him to me when he was weaned from his mother at eight weeks old. All of the other pups in the litter were trained and sold. My family had raised, trained, and sold German Shepherds for many years. They were great herding dogs and many of the farmers in our area had flocks of sheep and needed herding dogs to manage their flocks.

I enjoyed watching the dogs work the sheep. Even though they eyed the sheep intensely, it looked like they were having fun. Persistently focused, heads facing forward, eyes alert, crouching low, they purposefully watched for an opportunity to rush in and collect their brood of complaining animals. They'd gather them in a pen, or help us move them to a different pasture. Moving the sheep was an enjoyable job for the dogs, and one they looked forward to.

Basil was supposed to be a herding dog as well. However, he was born with a deformed back paw, walked with an unusual gait and couldn't be sold.

I pleaded with my father, "Please, papa, don't put him down. He won't be any trouble, I promise."

"Ewa, we can't keep pups that won't sell."

A chunk of disagreement stood between us. To my father it was a business, that's all, but to me it was so much more. I was so attached to this tiny pup with the funny back paw that I ignored my papa's reasoning and treated him with all the love and care I could give him. I just couldn't leave him alone. Every spare minute I had was spent holding and playing with him. Whenever I entered the kennel, he was the first to bound over and greet me. He was comfortable in my arms. After playing, I'd sit and hold him. He often slept on his back in the crook between my body and my arm, legs moving, chasing squirrels in his dreams. I begged grandpa to talk with my papa about him. I'd never wanted anything so badly before, and I couldn't imagine not seeing him every day. I didn't recognize it then, but I was learning about love and survival; how they often go hand in hand, like storks and Poland.

Even though he wasn't perfect, he was perfect to me, so I named him Basil. His alertness and knowing gaze always reminded me of how strong, smart, sensitive, and loyal he was. He remained by my side from the first day I got him. Despite my father's misgivings and my mother's protests, he slept on the floor next to my bed. I fell asleep every night rubbing his ear and woke every morning to see his head resting on the edge of my bed, his eyes focused on my face, waiting patiently for me to open mine. Basil, my shadow, accompanied me wherever I went, even school. He lay outside the classroom door, eagerly waiting for me to emerge and take my place beside him on the walk home. In the early fall we'd stop and pick the "paper" apples off the trees that grew along the road. They were delicious, white-fleshed balls of taste. They made the best applesauce and Basil loved them as much as I did, except he ate every part, seeds and core included.

Basil was my constant companion and best friend. When he wanted my attention he'd lay his head on my arm, and if that didn't work he'd take tiny pinch-like bites on my arm, or lean all his weight on my leg. On days when I didn't go to school I'd finish my chores, and we'd take off exploring parts of the farm and the forest beyond. Daily as spring approached, we'd journey to the meadow and the wooden gate so I could look for the first stork.

I told him things I couldn't tell anyone else. His sympathetic eyes reassured me that he was listening, and understood how I felt. I was safe with Basil by my side. Unlike me, he was quick to pick up unusual sounds and smells, and to notice small differences in our everyday world. If he could have talked, he would have warned me about the German invasion and complete destruction of my country. Perhaps I placed too much trust in him but life was changing so quickly that spring and summer, and I needed something constant to hold on to. Basil was all those things and more.

* * *

A slight gust of wind hit the barrack, bringing me back to the plain, wooden walls and the desolation of Litzmannstadt. No paint, no color, no pictures, just one small window that scarcely let any light in. It was such a severe contrast to my bedroom at home. Though small, it was cozy and colorful. The walls were bright yellow, and the morning light gave it a sunny glow on cloudy days. The timbered walls here were rough and thin, and barely kept the wind out. In winter it was a freezing ice-box, in summer hot like an oven.

I was saddened to realize how familiar this all felt to me now. Looking around I wondered if I would ever go home and feel my parents' hugs, Basil's licking kisses, or smell my grandma's baking. The starkness of this place made my memories more alive, staring me down like a persistent herding dog, refusing to let me forget where I came from, keeping me focused on where I needed to go. Some days it felt as though it would be easier to give up, but the memories wouldn't let me. "Hang on," they whispered.

"I am," my heart responded, ashamed I'd entertained any thought of giving up.

This camp had seen far too many children come and go, who like myself had left families, pets and homes behind. Were their memories as distinct as mine? There was never time to talk in the mornings. We worked for twelve hours every day. In the evenings, exhausted, starved, ready to collapse, we shared a few stories, but fatigue and hunger settled in like a heavy bank of fog, its weight lulling us to sleep. Sleep meant we'd survived another day. Sleep meant we'd have an opportunity to dream. Sleep meant escape from the cruel and harsh realities of war and life in a labor camp. Sleep was never long enough.

Chapter 4

Wisdom

The nests are constructed of branches and sticks and lined with twigs, grasses, leaves, rags, and paper. Stork nests are very strong, enduring for long periods of time. Some nests have been in continuous use for hundreds of years.

Wisdom is the ability to grasp things intuitively, and beyond that, to use the knowledge you've gained with decency. Animals often have an innate wisdom, a set of abilities they are born with, knowing intuitively how to do many things without being taught. Knowledge is different than wisdom and can be used to help people or hurt them. That's where the decency comes in, connecting knowledge to goodness.

I suppose from the outside looking in, this place was lacking in wisdom and decency. If you were standing outside our camp, what would you expect to see? Skinny, dirty souls that shuffled to and from their worksites in robotic movement? Wisdom and dignity for the Nazis was far different from wisdom and dignity for the inmates. Wisdom for us meant basic survival. Wisdom was about observing rules and working hard; paying attention to the behavior and moods of the guards, and staying out of their way. An unspoken rule for us was "don't stand out" but sometimes, even that didn't guarantee absolute success. As the war progressed some of the guards became more lenient, while others became more vicious, making our routines a complicated maze of uncertainty.

Dignity was shown in small acts of selflessness between the inmates. These were acts the guards were mostly unaware of. Offering a quick hug, sharing part of your bread, offering a smile or a hurried grasp of someone's hand, a wink, a private joke, a song from home. It was never big or showy, but it often had a profound effect on me. We all had good and bad days. More often than not, the small dignities we afforded one another kept us going, especially on the days we found ourselves running low on memories, or seeing any light in the world we now found ourselves enslaved in.

* * *

Some girls were starting to stir and awaken. A few girls were quietly whispering. I was reminded of my parents' hushed conversations in the days leading up to the war. They knew the situation in our country was grave, but I doubt they knew, or could have begun to imagine, the brutality and force of the German invasion. How could we have known that Poland would be gone in thirty days? You can't wrap your mind around that kind of evil; it's too big and impossible to understand. While my parents whispered, my mind flooded with questions. *Would Germany really attack us? What would become of us if there was a war? Would it be as the boys at school said, with German soldiers turning around and running from the Polish army? What would happen to my family, Basil, and the farm animals?* Unfortunately, I now knew the answers to all of those questions and even a few others I hadn't thought of.

During the months leading up to September in 1939, my parents and grandparents tried to reassure me that we'd be alright, all of us...but their faces told a different story. Their normal calm demeanor was replaced with a seriousness that scared and worried me. I longed for the pre-war quiet that cradled us and made us feel secure. I began to notice missing items; the silver frame that held my parents' wedding picture, the beveled mirror that my mother spent so much time polishing, the hand crocheted table cloth for our Sunday dinners after Mass, and the crystal vase that my grandfather had given my grandmother for one of their wedding anniversaries. Was my mother hiding them or selling them? Why would she do either if we were going to be alright? My father would leave our home after dinner and walk to the woods that bordered our farm. *Where was he going?* After I'd gone to bed, I'd hear him arrive home late, exhaustion mirrored in his heavy steps. My mother and grandparents spoke softly to him in muffled tones; conversations cloaked in anxiety and despair.

Suddenly my parents were warning me: "Ewa, don't go too far!"

"Come back quickly when we call!"

"Don't wander off the paths!"

I knew this land like the back of my hand. I'd traveled these forest paths my whole life. I knew most of its plants, trees, animals, and secret places. I knew the different trees; which ones were hard wood and which ones were soft, which trees provided fencing and those my papa used for fuel. I knew which plants to avoid and those I could touch.

Unfortunately, my skill in the forest didn't change their concern. They'd become even more concerned about my wandering the farm and surrounding forest. I was perfectly capable outdoors; I had an innate affinity with nature, stronger than any friendship bond, and a comfortableness that unsettled them now that we were going to war. They knew Basil was with me. Maybe, our proximity in the German countryside made them nervous; after all, we were no longer in our country, but in the middle of theirs. I was too afraid to ask my mother about the things I saw. Anxiety furrowed her brow, and increased her sighs; I didn't want to add to her concerns or make her voice the ones already consuming her.

I did talk to Basil though, on our walks around the farm. When I was finally quiet and worn out from the worry, he'd head off and find something. He'd bring it to me, dropping it at my feet; a goose feather, a pine cone, an unusual rock. He'd probably have brought me a squirrel if he could have caught one. I guess he was trying to make up for the things that were disappearing from my home and life. I saved all of his gifts in a box under my bed.

I wished I had them under the wooden bunk I slept in now. Hugging him always made me feel safe, a feeling that I visited often in my dreams; but now, that feeling was as foreign as a full meal, or kindness from the guards. At night, while drifting off to sleep, I would reach into my coat pocket and rub the cluster of coarse dog hair I'd accidentally pulled out of Basil when the soldiers ripped me away from him. I tried to pretend it was his ear and that I was rubbing it like I did before all this madness took my world away. That cluster of Basil's hair was one more thing the Germans couldn't take from me. I'd kept it carefully hidden, along with my memories. It wasn't impossible to keep things hidden from the guards, but it was challenging, and always risky.

I wasn't the only one keeping things hidden. Mama had kept her concerns hidden from me as well. She seemed to be preparing me for survival, a mother bear teaching her cub how to ride out a storm. She reminded me of how strong I was. A few days before the German invasion, we were hanging laundry on our clothesline. There was a slight breeze blowing, infusing our sheets with freshness. I loved crawling into fresh, crisp sheets at night. She asked me if I remembered the song she'd taught me to sing when I'd had a bad dream. It was a song about the moon. She told me that after she'd taught me the song, I'd never woken her again, but sometimes she'd heard me singing softly in the middle of the night. She held my face gently in her hands, and gazed into my eyes before speaking the next words.

"Ewa, I don't want to frighten you, but if we should get separated in the war I want you to think about all those little things, and cling to them, because they will bring you safely back to me."

"I will mama, I promise. Don't worry, mama, we'll be ok. We have papa, grandpa, and Basil to protect us."

She quickly bent down and grabbed another sheet out of the laundry basket. I could see her eyes tearing up, but couldn't figure out why.

* * *

I lay back down. The siren hadn't called us to work yet, so there was no need to rush it. Back on my bunk, I quietly hummed the song about the moon. I looked out the narrow window and my heart filled with love for my family. Just as a young stork leaves its nest but continues to be fed by its parents, I would continue to be fed by recollections of mine.

I whispered, "Mama, I'm staying strong like you taught me." I knew wherever she and papa were, they would be so proud of me.

Chapter 5

Understanding

Adult white storks are about three feet tall, with long red legs, a straight pointed red bill, white plumage, and black wing feathers.

Understanding happens when wisdom and experience collide. Many of the children in this camp were aware of the fragile nature of their existence. Many had understanding beyond their years. They had learned to survive and adapt to one of the harshest environments imaginable. A natural pecking order developed in each barrack with younger or newer inmates following the lead of those who'd been here the longest.

From the outside looking in, you wouldn't see how we'd obtained understanding. You would only notice the dirtiness of our appearance, the thinness of our bodies. You wouldn't be able to see the hearts in our chests that had survived starvation, beatings, kidnapping, and desolation. You wouldn't see the determination to survive in our eyes, because our downward gaze kept that knowledge from our captors. You wouldn't see the thoughts we clung to every day: *Soon this war will end and we will go home...soon.*

Circumstances had taught us that not all children in the world get to experience life through the joy of childhood. We learned that being Polish at this moment in time meant living a life that was out of our control, the life of an inmate in a labor camp. It was the opposite of a joy-filled childhood.

* * *

I could hear some finches singing outside the window. It was steadily growing lighter and the beautiful songs of the birds were a bitter contrast to the life we were living. We were Polish, we were Catholic, we were children, and we were slaves. We were the brown haired, brown eyed children who didn't resemble the German race enough in hair and eye color to be considered for Germanization. By Hitler's orders, all others were to become slave laborers or exterminated.

Our first camp was a youth labor camp that had once been a boarding school.

It was almost completely surrounded by high walls so it was difficult to look out, except on one side. From there, despite the barbed wire fencing, we had a clear view of the area surrounding us. There was farmland with patches of trees; fields of beets, potatoes, grasses, nature, and in the distance was a town. Work details gave us a limited view of the ghetto, but the scenery surrounding the ghetto was open to us and provided my soul the view of nature it desperately hungered for.

I'd always been aware of how much I valued nature and scenery, perhaps because it reminded me of my family's farm. Though I never could have guessed that its view would be withheld from me at any point in my life. Now it was such a treat to look at nature, and understand that its beauty held a deeper meaning; it was symbolic of life, sustenance, and creation. I wondered what had lived here before the ghetto and the labor camp. The ghetto couldn't have possibly looked like it did now. No one would have wanted to live there.

The run-down section of town, known as the Lodz ghetto, was particularly unsettling. It had the appearance of a living ghost town. There was no color. People lived there, but it appeared lifeless. It was comprised of buildings instead of barracks, but everything from the buildings, to the inhabitants' clothes, to the faces of the people, was dirty, drab and malnourished… ash-like, as if its fire had burned out and gray embers were all that remained in front of us. It was always so oddly quiet too, like the sounds of living had been sucked out of the air; just breathing was hard enough. Even though we only walked on its border streets, it terrified me to walk near it. Occasionally, on my way to the factory, I would witness the blank stares of the inhabitants. Ignoring their looks of desperation and their struggle to stay alive was impossible. Those feelings would stay with me long after leaving the area. In my heart, it was impossible to understand how one hate-filled mind could create so much misery and destroy so many lives.

Thousands of Polish children had been ripped away from their families and sent to orphanages and private homes in Germany to "learn" to be German. As Hitler ordered, their Polish culture and heritage was to be completely wiped out of their hearts and memories. These children were considered suitable for Germanization only if they met the physical qualifications, learned the German language, and disregarded their Polish culture and memories.

When Germany invaded Poland, their intent was to completely destroy our country; families, homes, businesses, and churches. They believed the Polish people were inferior to the German race. They waged war on our government, our people and our culture. Those who were old or sick would be killed and all others would provide slave labor to support Germany in its efforts to dominate the world. Our land was given to support Hitler's ideal of a pure Aryan race.

Our camp was officially called the Polish Youth Detainment Camp. It housed children for various reasons. Not all of us in this camp failed the physical examinations. Some children were here because they were caught stealing food, a necessary survival skill as the war dragged on. Others had been displaced because of the war, or convicted of some minor infraction. Still others had unwillingly been given to the Germans because their parents hoped they would qualify for Germanization, and this designation would save their child's life. How fitting that the one thing that sustained me, my memory, was the one thing Hitler insisted his Germanized children lose.

We ranged in age from five to sixteen, but most of us looked younger. We were so small from never having enough to eat. In fact, our days were divided up by the meal times. We existed on two meals a day of watery soup and sometimes, if we were lucky, stale bread. Occasionally, if we were out working on a farm, we would steal anything we could to fill our shriveled stomachs; grass, raw vegetables, even grain that was supposed to be for the animals. It didn't matter to us as long as we had something to put in our stomachs. All of our waking thoughts seemed to be about food, but our constant fear was getting caught, which meant a severe beating or even death for stealing needed food. We were constantly reminded how fortunate we were to receive two meals a day! The soldiers told us that other camps gave one meal a day and sometimes nothing. Although this desolate place didn't remotely resemble home, I knew it had to be better than one of the concentration camps. In my mind though, it was difficult to distinguish between them. Prison was prison. Different degrees of difficulty existed in each, but all were formed for the same purpose to achieve Hitler's goal of world domination, and enslave anyone he viewed as standing in the way of his objectives.

Like Basil used to be, hunger became my constant companion. My family and Basil were daily in my thoughts. *Were they alive? Were they ok? Where were they and would we ever see each other again?*

When I was assigned to work on a farm out in the countryside I became very homesick. I thought about our farm; like the River Warta in the spring overflowing her banks, my mind flooded with questions. I wondered about the people using our farm to produce food and animals for Germany. I couldn't bear the thought of our farm supporting Hitler, nor of a German family using our home, supporting his Aryan ideals and programs for developing his "Master Race".

I feared my parents and grandparents had been taken to a labor camp. Anyone who appeared healthy could be deported at any time. I tried not to visualize how they were managing, especially if they were separated. I knew that elderly people, as well as the very young and infirm, were usually viewed as useless. I knew my grandparents were strong and capable of working long hours. Perhaps the soldiers would consider their usefulness as well as their age.

Concern for our loyal, hardworking German Shepherds came often to my mind. We had trained them to herd sheep. We cared for them lovingly. Were they now performing sentry duty and living in kennels? The thought of them being mistreated or handled roughly by soldiers made me feel down. I was sure the Germans treated the dogs better than the children who slaved for them, though. I did not believe anyone could be more mistreated than us. One of the older girls, however, insisted that we weren't treated as badly as the Jews. As we were barely surviving, I wondered how anyone could survive harsher conditions. The thought of harsher treatment sent chills down my spine. I couldn't entertain such a thought; I'd survived this long, and I wanted to see the end of the war. I wanted to go home and feel the warmth of my mama's embrace and the strength of my papa's arms. I wanted to smell my grandmother's freshly baked bread and hear my grandfather's silly sayings and songs, and I desperately wanted to wrap my arms around Basil's neck and feel the warmth of his shiny coat and the wetness of his tongue licking my cheek. A slight breeze, carrying a leaf from a nearby tree, got my attention, and brought me back to the task at hand, weeding the beet and potato fields. I paused from working to look at the rows of vegetables growing. I was surrounded by fields of food that we would be harvesting in a couple of months, but none of it would be given to us. This realization caused a tear to drop from my eye; I quickly wiped it away. I'd always remembered the admonition Berta had given me on my arrival: "Don't ever let them see you cry, it only makes them angry....don't give them the opportunity to beat you!"

Berta had passed all the tests for Germanization. A child's suitability for being racially valuable was based on measurements of sixty-two parts of their bodies. The Nazis were looking for specific characteristics. A child's hair and eye color, the shape of their nose and lips, the hairline, the toe and fingernails; all these things determined if they would be chosen. They also had to pass neurological tests, IQ tests, and they were watched closely for personal habits such as bed-wetting and nail biting. If they had any of these habits they were rejected even though they had passed all of the other tests. They were forbidden to speak Polish. They were given German names, issued false birth certificates, drafted into Nazi youth groups, and instructed in German language, geography, and history lessons every day. If they didn't conform they were starved or beaten and eventually sent to a labor or extermination camp. The Nazis found it so easy to disregard a human life. They never saw beyond the outward appearance to what existed inside.

Berta had been taken by the Nazis when she was eleven. She didn't last long in the Germanization program because she stubbornly embraced her culture, language and memories. She refused to forget who she was and where she had come from, as well as her native tongue. Whenever she was found singing a Polish song, she was severely beaten, but it never deterred her from remembering who she really was. Eventually, they tired of her stubbornness and she was sent to our labor camp, her memories and culture too strong to be abandoned.

Berta was one of the few children I could completely trust. Her dislike of Germany was as strong as her love of Poland. Her parents had earned their living by crafting beautiful wooden boxes and hope chests. Her father had learned the trade from his family. The designs had been passed down from generation to generation for years. They lived in southern Poland in the Carpathian Mountains, near the Slovakian border.

During one of our lunch breaks, I noticed her drawing designs in the dirt with a stick. Thinking she was playing a game I asked her if I could play.

She shyly looked up at me and whispered, "Just watch."

Design after design appeared in the dirt like magic. Triangles, circles and lines blended into beautiful designs that I couldn't imagine ever creating myself.

"What are they for, eggs?"

Berta shook her head and I continued to watch as she effortlessly continued drawing.

I was familiar with the Pisanki eggs available in Kostrzyn at Easter time, and even though these designs were similar, they weren't quite the same.

It wasn't until several days later, during another work break, that Berta told me about her parents and the Polish crafts they made and sold for a living. It was hard for her to talk about them without tearing up. I could tell she thought about her parents as often as I thought about mine. I softly squeezed her hand, and told her to always keep them in her heart. That way she'd never lose them, and no one could ever really take them from her.

She nodded her head and said, "Yes, I suppose that's true, but somehow I'd feel better if I could touch them and hear them."

I didn't know what to say to her. Words couldn't fix the years of injustice, cruelty, and ravage of our lives and country. The awkward suggestion spilled out of me despite my misgivings.

"You will again soon, Berta."

"How can you be so sure, Ewa? Especially when we don't see any end in sight?"

"You heard what the underground is telling us. The Germans are losing the war, Russia has turned against them, and they are no longer allies."

"I hope they are telling us the truth, Ewa. I don't know how much longer I can stand living like this."

"I know what you mean. On days when I'm sad, I pick out a day from before the war. It could be a special day, like a holiday. I try to recall every detail from that day...the weather, people, food we ate, things we did, smells, colors, special activities, the clothes we wore... I try to remember every little detail. Then I know I'll have it in my memory forever, and it is one more thing the Germans can't take away from me. Think about all the days you spent living before the war, Berta. How you may have watched or helped your mama make breakfast, or work on her craft work. Did you help select trees in the forest for their crafts? What did you see as you hiked in the woods? What did you hear, smell, and feel? You can never forget those things."

"I was always in trouble for remembering those things in the Germanization Program, Ewa."

"Yes, but not here. Here the only thing they care about is how hard we work. They've already decided we aren't good enough to be German. Here, we are just slaves, and as long as we work we can think whatever we want to think. I like to think about home and going back there sometime soon."

Our short break was over. The rows of crops, like obedient soldiers, stood at attention waiting for our stewardship. The guards started yelling at us to get back to work. Berta nodded her head. I could tell our conversation had started her thinking about the differences between our labor camp and the Germanization program. Even though both took away independence, in some ways we had more freedom here; we could speak Polish among ourselves, and remember who we were. Usually we'd find an opportunity to share a memory with one another, and feed our souls in a way that food never could. It was more than knowledge, facts or ideas. It was the gift of wisdom, discerning how the memory strengthened our resolve to survive. It enabled us to make important comparisons, and changed our focus from barely hanging on, to survival for a reason – the opportunity to regain our lives and families.

I picked up my tool and started working the ground again. It felt good to be out in the fresh air and sunshine. My hands were calloused and hard and didn't blister anymore from this kind of work. I was good at telling the difference between the weeds and the crops that were growing. I was trying to figure out when I could sneak one of the young beets out of the ground and into my mouth when I saw the transport trucks pulling up to the gates.

A shiver came over me causing me to tremble involuntarily. My heart started beating faster and my palms began sweating. Another load of terrified children peeked out between the thick boards in the back of the trucks. Like sheep being hauled to market, their eyes pleaded, hoping for relief from the confusion and chaos they were now part of. Who would give them comfort and ease their uncertainty and fear? Penned up like animals, they waited for the guards to open the barbed wire gate. I shuddered at the memory of my arrival as my heart filled with compassion for the young ones being introduced to slavery. The guards did a good job of intimidating their distressed charges from the time they stepped off the transport trucks. If being exhausted, disoriented, starved and weak wasn't enough, they yelled at them, allowing their dogs to lunge, bark, and snarl. If they didn't move fast enough to the shower building they would swear at them and call them names and whack them with sticks. It was horrible to hear the terrified screams of the children. I recalled the playground sign from the German school I'd imagined: "No Playing Allowed...fight, fight, fight." Yes, the Nazis were experts at wounding children. I prayed that God would let this madness end soon. I looked at the dirt and fought back the tears burning my eyes. Injustice, terror, slavery, there were no good words to describe what the Nazis had done. There were no good reasons either. There was only one ultimate aim of German policy toward the Polish children: biological reduction- by Germanization, enslavement and extermination.

Sadly, I turned my back on the screams and cries of children. My stomach rolled like a ball was bouncing around inside of it. I leaned over and retched but nothing came out. A cold sweat broke out on my forehead. I bent over, panting, awaiting relief from the nausea. My racing heart slowed, as the sickness began to subside. It was terrifying being on the receiving end of Nazi bullying, but for me it was even harder bearing witness to the cries of innocent children being mistreated.

The Germans had succeeded in at least one way – we'd become like animals working on the instinct of survival. Everything we did was governed by our desire to survive. It was tiring to monitor my behavior all the time. All that was expected of me here was work and obedience, nothing more. So I was presented with a problem; how did I turn off caring for others, showing kindness, sharing with people, celebrating, compassion, anger and love. I constantly had to pay attention so I wouldn't cross the line and react and be seen as a threat. Wisdom and experience had collided.

The storks instinctively forage for food in loose, large groups of birds, but that was their innate nature. How I longed to pay attention to the thoughts and feelings of my nature as well as my instincts. *Soon,* I reminded myself, *my life will come back to me. It can't go on like this forever.*

Chapter 6

Rescue

Breeding birds add to the nest each summer, with both males and females contributing to the construction.

Often, after days of working the fields, I'd awake with dirt-crusted eyes. This morning, as I struggled to open them I could hear the dogs whining outside our barrack, eager to enter and bark their commands, warning the children to get busy. Within seconds the guards, along with their dogs, would be entering, shouting at us to wake up, eat our soup, and go outside for roll call. I was so relieved to be awake already because I hated the days when I was sleeping deeply, dreaming of my life before the war, only to be abruptly torn from my dreams by the sound of yelling. The hollering was all done in German with the soldiers acting as if we couldn't understand them. They acted as if screeching loudly increased comprehension.

What most of the guards didn't discern, however, was that in my town, Kostrzyn, I had many, many German neighbors. We were so close to the border that numerous German families had settled in the area over the years. I had learned German as a young girl; my father had insisted on it. The breeding stock that my father used for his dogs was from Germany. Many of his business dealings were conducted in German and I went with him whenever possible. The German families I had grown up with had children that went to our schools. They shopped in our town and even went to our churches. It was hard for me to imagine them being my neighbor one minute and my enemy the next. I wondered if they really hated me as much as their government told them they should.

Hitler had gone to great lengths to legalize a number of

repressive measures in a law he proclaimed as the "Law for the Protection of German Blood and Honor." It simply meant the German people wanted to keep their blood pure and their culture together, so no marriages of mixed race. He turned his racial ideologies into laws that created enemies of other cultures. Other countries simply existed to support the Aryan ideals of Adolf Hitler. It seemed odd to me that Hitler valued his culture so much, yet felt the need to destroy everyone else's.

The soldiers stormed in, yelling as usual while directing their dogs to bark us awake. It wasn't enough for them to merely startle us awake; they thrived on terrorizing us. The commotion was always unsettling but especially so if you were sound asleep. One of the newer, younger girls was so startled by the commotion that she started screaming. Eyes wide with fear, she clutched her coat and curled up in the corner of the bunk trying to escape. This only made the dogs bark more ferociously. I wanted to go help her but feared the consequences of stepping in. I knew how to handle dogs, and I also knew that if you showed any fear, the dogs would sense it and feel like they had the upper hand. I searched my brain for some way to step in and not be considered disobedient. The young girl's terrified screaming was making my heart race with fear for her. All of the other girls had cleared out of the barrack as fast as possible, so only this young girl, the Germans, and I remained. I eyed the young German that was handling the more aggressive of the two dogs. He seemed unsure of how to gain control of the situation.

All of the snarling, lunging and barking was only making the tiny, terrified child retreat farther back into her bunk. She rolled herself into a tight ball in an attempt to escape, but her screaming was keeping the dogs agitated. Suddenly I heard the word *"enough"* escape through my lips. I'd said it in German, the way my father had taught me to when I needed to take command of a misbehaving dog. The force and loudness that I'd said it with, surprised not only me, but the guards and the attacking dogs, who not only obeyed me but suddenly sat by their masters' uniformed legs and looked at me as if waiting for another command.

I quickly spoke again in German. "I'll take her out...stupid girl, she was really agitating the dogs."

I wanted them to think I was on their side, and that I hadn't crossed the line and forgotten my place. I ran down to the bunk and quickly grabbed the sobbing bundle, yanking her by the back of her tattered coat. I pulled and her body slid backward off the wooden bunk, legs unfolding in the air. Thankfully, she landed on her feet. I grabbed her hand and started running down the aisle of the barrack toward the door.

We were going to make it. I couldn't believe it.

We were just stepping outside when I heard the word, "HALT."

Chapter 7

Grace

Storks stay with one mate for the breeding season, but they do not migrate or over-winter together.

I could hear the heels of his boots hitting the floor with authority as he walked toward us. He was smacking his heels so loudly I thought the wooden floor boards would crack. The little girl I'd rescued looked up at me, eyes pleading, nose running, grasping my hand so tightly my fingers pinched. Her dirty face, stained from tears, reminded me of how terrified I felt when I first arrived here. The loudness and smells of the camp along with the starkness of the barracks were unsettling, and I knew how intimidated she felt. I gave her hand two quick squeezes to let her know we'd be ok.

"You two turn around," he commanded.

Time stood still as we slowly turned, dropping our grasp, then grabbing hands again once we were around and facing the soldier and his dog. I could feel my heart pounding my chest while my breath panted noisily in my ears. My stomach growled so loudly I feared the soldiers would hear it and get angry. We didn't dare look at the soldiers. I stared at his shiny black boots polished to perfection. The sight of the dogs sitting so closely made the tiny girl begin to whimper and she started sliding behind me.

"Naa, naa, shhh," I quickly said. "You'll get them barking again."

She stopped crying and peeked out from behind me, eyeing the dogs suspiciously.

The soldier leaned in so closely that I could smell his breath; sausage and cigarettes. I could also smell his dislike for us; his need to be done with us. In his eyes, we weren't worth the trouble we were causing. The annoyance flew from his mouth like a flock of starlings, thick, black, roiling. We were keeping him from accomplishing his list of duties for the day. Unlike his black boots, we weren't perfect. I knew I had placed myself in a very precarious situation, possibly changing my chance of survival. I may regret this impulsive choice.

The soldier spoke to me in German.

"Your little friend appears to be afraid of dogs, yes?"

I nodded yes. I hadn't meant to speak in German earlier, it just sort of happened; now he knew I could understand him.

"What is her name?" he asked.

I shrugged, then cautiously offered, "She is new to the camp and I haven't had time to get to know her yet."

"Ask her."

In Polish I quickly told her not to be afraid and asked her for her name.

"Anna," she replied in a shaky whisper.

"Anna," I repeated loudly so the soldier could hear. I didn't want the dog to think he was in charge so I tried to make myself stand as straight and tall as I could.

He continued. "But you, you're not afraid of dogs, are you?"

"No," I responded without volunteering any further information.

"What is your name?"

"Ewa," I said calmly.

"Ewa," he repeated in his German accent. "You should teach your little friend how to get up on time in the morning, no more of this nonsense, yes?"

"Yes," I replied.

"Now hurry or you'll be late for roll call."

We turned, and hands still clasped tightly, ran out of the building, and down the shadowed alley between the barracks. We stepped out into the broad, barren, wire-enclosed yard and quickly found a space in which to stand at attention. I couldn't believe we'd been able to run away unharmed from our encounter with the soldiers.

My heat beat started to slow its racing pace. In hindsight, I realized I'd just crossed a troll's bridge and survived without paying a toll. Or had I?

Good, they hadn't started roll call yet. Anna was shivering. In strong, crisp German, the commander of the camp was going over camp rules again and talking about the importance of doing our best for Germany. The vocabulary from his mouth was so exact, so sharp; instead of paying attention to his message, I marveled at the perfection of each syllable in each word. I imagined him being a language professor before the war; leading his students in speaking drills with precise pronunciation. Dressed in perfectly polished shoes, clothes cleaned and ironed to perfection, walking up and down the rows of desks, keeping tempo with a pointer smacking his hand in perfect time, and laying it against the ear of anyone brazen enough to become distracted and speak off tempo. Perfection demanding perfection from those around him.

His monthly tirades about camp rules were so familiar that instead of listening I let my thoughts roam freely, dreaming about my life before the war. Then I heard him say something that brought me right back to reality. The Red Cross was coming for a visit and we were starting a camp beautification program.... today. He informed us that we would be helping with that process.

I was unsure what that meant. Could it possibly mean more food for us? Even if it was just for a day, the thought of something more to eat sounded beyond wonderful. Would we be able to actually speak with the Red Cross delegates, or would the Germans keep us hidden in the woods somewhere? Maybe we would get new straw mattresses and blankets. I could never have guessed the depths of deception the Nazis would go through in their attempt to make the world think they were involved in treating children with dignity and respect. Still, I couldn't help feeling that the Red Cross visit was proof that we were not beyond help. We could walk out of here someday soon. *Please, please, let it be soon.* I eyed my bony legs. Thread-bare socks barely covered my ankles. Like slices of Swiss cheese, my shoes were riddled with holes. I needed to find rags to bind them and fill the holes. I was shivering from the brisk morning air. A new pair of shoes and socks for the Red Cross visit would be wonderful, but in all actuality, not very likely.

As the camp commander spoke on and on, the chilly morning air reminded me of how I used to attend similar assemblies in the mornings at my old school. At the start of every month our school principal used to speak to all the students about following school rules and doing our best on our school work. It must be the start of a new month. Suddenly, like a gust of wind, the thought hit me… *it must be April,* which meant I would soon see the storks again. It was a good day, a very good day. It amazed me how one single thought could suddenly change my whole world to a brighter place. Especially this place, with all of its sadness and suffering. As usual, the thought of seeing the storks lifted my mood.

Grandpa's words came back to me. *Wuroczystość Zwiastowaniabocian ma stanąć na jego gniazdo:* on the feast of the Annunciation a stork shall stand on its nest. *The storks are a blessing because they teach us to have faith.*

"Thank you, grandpa," I whispered. The Feast of the Annunciation always comes in the last week of March to commemorate the angel Gabriel telling Mary that she would be the mother of Jesus. The storks' arrival and the holy day were closely linked in our Catholic tradition as well as nature's timing.

Anna squeezed my hand with two quick movements then dropped it so we could put our arms obediently by our sides, like two small fish swimming with the current in a sea of chaos. It seemed that a sentry dog rescue was a great starting point to an enduring alliance. I took a deep breath, and I felt calm. I knew I could smell the earth waking from winter. I couldn't believe I'd managed to escape a beating. Usually, if you stepped in to help another child, you would receive a beating as well.

But a thought kept nagging me like a herding dog nipping an animal's heels. I worried that after the soldiers thought about it for a while they would come back and unleash their anger on me.

So far I'd managed to receive only one whipping; it was enough to keep me from ever purposely disobeying again. I asked a question... once. The guard, eyeing me with disgust and suspicion, took my inquiry as doubting his authority. He dragged me to the front of the work detail and beat me so badly that walking was difficult for days. My legs still bore the marks of his wrath.

I was shocked that this time. Not only had I'd kept Anna from getting beaten, I hadn't gotten one either. Even better though, I'd just gained a friend.

Grace is characterized by giving freely with goodness and love. I'd shown grace today; to a small frightened child. I felt like a giant, and my heart was bursting with a happiness that it hadn't known in a very long time.

Now, only one thing could make this day even better...seeing a stork. My mind wandered again to thoughts about their migration. *Where would they be in their long journey back to Poland?* Just because Poland no longer existed to the Nazis, didn't mean the storks recognized it as a different place. After all, they'd been coming here for hundreds of years. It was one part of our culture Hitler couldn't destroy.

Chapter 8

Shaken

The female stork usually lays three to five eggs, and both parents incubate the eggs for about one month. This group of eggs is referred to as a clutch.

For two days I was assigned to perform factory work; which meant working inside all day long, head down, shoulders aching, squinting in poor light at some metal object that belonged to a piece of German war equipment. I fantasized about the part I was working on; breaking down at a crucial moment and disabling the Nazis' plan for control and world domination.

My job was to assemble a few of the pieces together by lightly tapping them with a small metal hammer. Grab two pieces, tap them together, grab another, tap it on, and throw them in another box for the next girl on the line to pick up and work on…over and over and over. I fought the boredom by humming quietly to myself. I was so sleepy; I feared I was fighting a losing battle.

Briefly, I fell asleep, allowing the hammer to slip from my grasp and land on my foot. Toe throbbing, I quickly bent down, retrieved it and resumed assembling the metal discs. Humming wasn't going to work for me today, I needed to move if I was going to stay awake. Feet planted slightly apart, I gently rocked from side to side.

Now I could engage in my favorite pastime… daydreaming. Nothing about this setting sparked a memory for me. This job, with its senseless monotony of noise and repetition was not something I cared to focus on. Now, until the end of the day, could only be tolerated through the relief of memories. It would be nice to say that an endless supply of memories kept me from slipping into boredom and falling asleep on my feet again, but it didn't. The boredom, followed by the falling asleep happened again; only the difference was, it was witnessed by a guard.

I awoke, on my feet, to a big gray representative of the Nazi party. Though he was screaming at me, his German was barely audible, his words cushioned by the noise of the factory. He pelted me with threats and insults. By chance alone, it was a verbal assault, not one rained upon me by his hands or the butt of his rifle. I couldn't afford to get in trouble now; who would look after Anna? I quickly looked down and picked up the pace of my hammering. I desperately needed to be working outside. I cringed at the realization that I'd come very close to losing my life. In the late afternoon, the spring light filtered through the high windows on the factory walls, as dust filled sun rays beamed down, and I thanked God I'd been afforded a second chance.

Another young girl, two places from where I stood on the assembly line, hadn't been as fortunate as I. Amidst screamed promises of never falling asleep again, and cries of "I'm sorry," the child was dragged kicking and screaming to a transport truck and tossed in just as it was pulling out of camp. The gate sentries laughed at the monstrous act of the incensed guard. I could feel the panic rising in my chest; terror was paying me a visit today, but it was a visitor I didn't welcome. My fingers worked faster despite blurring tears pooling in my eyes.

Dear God, look after that child.

I hoped Anna was staying awake at whatever mindless task the Nazis had her doing today.

I thought about the young girl who'd been thrown out of the factory. How many times had she apologized on her way to transport? How many times had I apologized for real or imagined infractions against the Nazi regime?

"*I'm sorry* I took that breath of air."

"*I'm sorry* I fell asleep from exhaustion and starvation."

"*I'm sorry* I can't work harder and faster with less food and energy."

"*I'm sorry* I'm shivering from the cold."

There was a constant unspoken demand to apologize to our jailors. If we weren't sorry for staying alive the soldiers would remind us to be. I returned from the factory that day shaken but grateful.

The camp beautification program was in full swing now. Every day spent working outside the camp brought startling surprises upon our return. The dirt around the barracks had been raked into an orderly lined pattern. Not one weed could be spotted anywhere near the barracks. Doors were being painted different shades of dark colors. Potted flowering plants were even showing up on the edges of the barracks that rimmed the yard where we spent so much time standing at attention, receiving lectures and work orders.

During the last assembly, we'd been told that we needed to learn some songs, so we could entertain the visiting dignitaries. The commander informed us that we would start our music lessons soon. I couldn't imagine what songs they would be teaching us, and which, if any of the guards, had singing voices good enough to teach music to children. I never thought of the guards as people who might enjoy singing. I only heard them yell. The hollering started in the morning, continued throughout the day, and ended at night when we were in bed. I often wondered if that was the only way they communicated...by yelling. In my imagination I saw a small town in Germany where all the inhabitants yelled. They hollered their greetings, they screamed their goodbyes, but no one knew what anyone was saying because there was so much noise they couldn't hear! I smiled at the picture playing in my head. I suppose if you could holler, you could also sing.

The last time I sang in a choir was so long ago. The memory of it planted another smile on my face. Several Christmases back, I sang in the children's choir at church. I could carry a tune, but was genuinely shy when it came time to sing in front of anyone. On the day of the performance, instead of a small church with family and friends, the building suddenly took on gigantic proportions. The people-filled pews stretched as far as I could see. I didn't recognize anyone I knew in the rows and rows of faces staring at me. The room began to grow warm. Nervously, I took my place for the presentation, but didn't get the chance to perform. I stepped forward to sing my part; but something was wrong with my eyes. The words and notes swam around the page; the music didn't sound right, either. No singing was coming out of my mouth. My mouth was open, but my throat was dry. Sweat was rolling down my face and I had to keep wiping it away so I could read the music. Sensing my anxiety, the teacher had another child step in to sing my part. I stood there looking at my feet, afraid to move and draw any more attention to myself.

Wearing my disappointment like an old hat pulled low on my face, I stood while mama hugged me and told a story about the time she'd done the same thing as a child. My jaw ached from holding back the tears. Mama's hug took away the defeat and replaced it with empathy. Everything was good now, because her hug repaired the distress.

The beautification program was completing the many objectives in their plan. There were rumors of classrooms being constructed with actual desks, books, paper, and pencils. After dark, the barracks were buzzing with whispers about the changes coming our way. Excitement spilled over in the boys' barracks, causing a ruckus now and then, usually ending in some form of public humiliation. Too bad the Red Cross couldn't witness that.

Before the war, I wasn't very fond of school, but now it seemed like a good idea to sit in a desk, and listen to a teacher talk about science or geography or any subject for that matter. School was easy compared to twelve hours of work in a factory.

It wasn't a real school, but in this setting, during this time, you took what you could get. Even attending for a few weeks would be a welcome diversion from the repetition of factory work. More than likely, the school in our town was still open. However, not many of my old school friends, if any, were still living in Kostrzyn.

Plenty of funny stories from my school days waited to be plucked and dwelled upon. The exciting thing was until now, I hadn't really thought about them. I realized I had a whole new chapter from my past to entertain and sustain me.

After our country was attacked, families tried many different tactics to survive the war. Some left the country, some hid out in the woods, others stayed in their homes with the hope that they'd survive the onslaught. I could only envision the schools staying open to educate German children. In fact, according to Heinrich Himmler, a senior Nazi official, Polish children should be able to sign their own name, be obedient to the Germans and count to five-hundred, unless they passed Germanization tests. This designation meant education in the German language and subjects. Certainly no Polish teachers could remain; it was against Hitler's ideals.

Appearances were changing quickly in the camp. Berta told me that she saw huge loads of straw being dropped off at the rear of the camp. Maybe we were getting new mattresses! Our old, lice-infested straw mattresses would never pass an inspection by the Red Cross, and neither would our lice-infested bodies. They had to replace the mattresses and blankets if our bodies were going to look healthy. I wondered if the Red Cross could really be so easily fooled. I would soon realize how determined the Germans were to keep their secret hidden from the rest of the world.

One night during the frenzied whispering, someone mentioned that we would be having a stork festival like we used to have every year before the war. It was then I realized how resolved the Nazis were to hide their crimes and make the world see something completely opposite our everyday reality. We were hardly allowed to speak to one another during a regular work day, let alone sing, dance, put on a play and enjoy eating festive foods. Pickles, pirogues, honey cakes; all part of the holiday foods that were going to be served. My mouth watered at the thought of tasting those pleasurable dishes again. Could all these stories be true? Why would Germany put on a stork festival when Poland no longer existed in Hitler's Aryan nation? Storks were part of Poland's culture. I couldn't envision a festival celebrating one without honoring the other.

Anna had only been here for a few days, and I could already see her retreating further and further into herself. I felt so protective of her, I was afraid she was giving up. I needed and wanted to look after her, help her survive. She touched a place in my heart that made me feel like we were connected somehow, like she was the younger sister I'd longed for, who needed my strength and protection. The idea of a stork festival gave me something to discuss with her.

"Anna, did you and your family go to the stork festival in your town?"

"Yes, a few times."

"What was your favorite thing to do there?"

She didn't answer. She shrugged.

"I liked looking at all the crafts," I offered.

She looked down at the gray, lifeless dirt; her demeanor mirrored what her eyes were staring at. I'd have to keep trying. I knew the end of the war couldn't be too far off. The signs were everywhere and there were so many things I wanted to tell her. Things that could help her remember who she was, and that all of this craziness couldn't last forever. I reminded myself to go slow and not overwhelm her. Searching my brain for a way to connect with her, I wondered if she had a pet, or played a musical instrument. Maybe she was really good at schoolwork…there had to be something she would talk about.

"Time to leave with the work crew." Placing my hands on her head, I said, "Take care of yourself today, Anna, I'll see you tonight."

She slowly shook her head up and down. I quickly squeezed her hand goodbye. She was a girl, far from home, enslaved in a labor camp. It was easy to see the devastation she felt. Her fear of dogs may have been a blessing in disguise. That's what brought us together, forging a bond of protection and friendship. She needed me, but what she didn't understand was that I needed her, as well. I couldn't help notice the similarities. We'd both been rejected for Germanization. We were children, arriving here without siblings or someone to shield us from the brutality of this place. She was the younger sister I'd longed for my entire life. There was an acceptance and understanding between us. Words didn't need to be spoken because there were no cracks that needed to be filled with sound. Sometimes just being near someone is enough.

* * *

I was assigned to the factory again. Still, I had to acknowledge, while not as satisfying as farm work, at least it was better than stitching clothes or straightening needles. Sewing had never been something I enjoyed. Sewing came so easy to mama. She would make the most beautiful dresses and shirts. I watched with amazement as she stitched quickly and perfectly. She would patiently show me how to stitch seams by hand, but she knew I'd rather be outside running along the forest paths with Basil, or helping papa with chores.

Factory work also meant that I wouldn't get the opportunity to see the storks because I was inside all day. The sound of the factory was so deafening and tiring to hear for hours on end. The banging and clanging of metal along with the constant hum of machinery kept away all hope of hearing nature.

I longed for the sounds and sights of nature: wind blowing through trees, pigeons and cuckoos talking, pinecones tumbling through branches and hitting the ground with a muffled, forest-floor thud. The thrill of seeing birds play on the wind, gliding and diving, then coming back up to float in place for the slightest of seconds. I would wonder what it must be like to fly so freely. Sometimes if it was quiet enough at night I could even hear the ice, cracking apart on the pond near our camp, just like I used to hear it at home. From time to time during winter, I'd even hear an ice-covered branch crack and break free from the trunk, giving the tree a whole new shape and silhouette once its leaves returned. Unlike factory work, nature was never dull or boring. I would often lose all sense of time while walking through the trees near my home. Each season uncovered discoveries that thrilled me.

The forest and fields were beautiful in the spring. Red poppies and blue bachelor buttons would grow wild and sometimes you could find meadows filled with them. Lily of the valley grew at the edge of the forest. Little yellow buttercup plants called globeflowers grew along the streams and in the shady places of the woodland. The different kinds of trees wore a different jacket for each season, leaves and bark changing with the weather. Our woodlands were filled with oak, sycamore, and poplar interspersed with fir and pine. These different species afforded variety, and supported many kinds of wildlife. Beavers, deer and wolves were some of the animals inhabiting Poland's wetlands and thickets.

I loved picking wildflowers and pressing them. Grandmother taught me how to place them on the sheets of paper so they would dry in an attractive shape. My grandfather made me a flower press out of some thin, wood boards and a leather strap. I used layers of paper between the boards to soak up any moisture. After the flowers were pressed and dry, I glued them carefully in a book that had paper pages separated by wax sheets. I could spend hours looking for flowers to press; I rarely tired of it. Grandma would help identify them and tell me how they could be used.

Basil would keep himself busy by chasing small rodents while I picked flowers. Squirrels chattered at him as he ran from tree to tree. It almost sounded as if they were laughing at him. The memory of Basil chasing a squirrel from one tree to another brought a smile to my face because I knew he wouldn't know what to do with one if he did catch it. He was so gentle; even to the point of entering the chicken coop with me to sit calmly and watch as I collected eggs, he never upset the hens.

In some measure, with farm work I had the chance to be outside, to breathe fresh, clear air; it wasn't as free as wandering through the forest back home, but at least I was outside. The hardest part about being here, aside from missing my family and home so desperately, was being close to the trees and yet so forbidden to walk through them, touching, smelling, and looking at the abundance of life. I longed to see the woodpeckers, bitterns and warblers, as well as the squirrels and other small animals who made the forest their home. Looking out at the marsh I would see the older storks standing and preening the heads of the younger birds. Those days with Basil by my side, watching the storks and walking on our land, returned to me regularly in my dreams at night. Those dreams gave me strength. They reminded me that the Germans could take everything away, except the most important thing – my thoughts and dreams; I would go to my grave before letting them take those from me.

Chapter 9

Change

Young chicks are covered with white down and have black bills; their legs and bills slowly turn red as they mature.

Finally, after two days that seemed unreasonably long, I wasn't called for factory work. I took a deep breath of the crisp, daylight sky. It smelled so wet and earthy. I'd asked the other girls at night after returning from the fields if they'd seen any storks, but they just shook their heads *no*. They were so tired from working outside all day long and couldn't understand why I would rather be outside than inside a warm factory – even if it was noisy, at least it was warm, they reasoned. I was certain the storks would be here soon. The trees were showing all the signs. I was hopeful I'd see them today while working outside.

The joy and happiness I felt about being outside was not something I could explain to them. I only knew that when I first came to this camp I missed the big things; my family, my home, my church, and my community. With the passing of days and years, I still missed the big things, but began to miss more and more of the little things. It was like the memories broke down and opened up, and I could remember very small specific things: like the way our kitchen smelled in the morning when I woke up, or how snow coated the trees in our yard in the winter. I recalled the way church smelled upon entering; like burning candles, polished wood, and incense, as well as the way my first breath of fresh air felt when I left school at the end of the day.

I realized that those "big things" were made up of the dozens of little things that gave them meaning, life, and substance. Working on the farm only made those memories more distinct in my mind. I could pretend that I was home on my own farm. I think the Germans thought they were the only ones benefiting from my labor. Little did they know how much I appreciated the special memories that working outside afforded me.

In a strange way, I knew that life couldn't go on like this forever. Even though we were children, we were starting to see the breakdown of the German war machine. The Polish underground was active and involved in undermining the Nazis at every opportunity they found.

Rocks with notes attached would find their way to our feet when we were standing out in the yard. It was the most astonishing thing to be surrounded by inmates, barbed wire, guards on duty and almost be hit by a flying rock with a note. Berta received many of these "rocks" and would cautiously share their contents with the older inmates. Messages were never shared with the new inmates because trust hadn't been established yet.

It was like having the most wonderful secret. We just needed to make sure and keep the secret to ourselves. I had a running commentary playing in my head, updating any new information I received.

"The Germans are weakening daily in their efforts to control the world. The front is closing in with the help of the Polish underground. The Soviets have turned on the Nazis and soon they will rush back to Germany with their tail between their legs, proving once again that Poland is the stronger country."

Anna brightened when I whispered parts of the commentary, a slight smile gracing her face. Our lives here were nothing more than mere routine, colorless tasks. Sometimes, I wondered if the Nazis couldn't starve and work us to death, they would challenge our hope of survival by enforcing monotonous routines. I had to find ways to entertain myself and Anna – even turning a war report into a commentary helped relieve the boredom some.

Other than the rocks, there were a few ways we received information. The most common was when new groups of children arrived. We had an organized way of finding out what new children might know about the war, and life outside the camp. We would ask them specific questions. If they answered in a particular way we'd know if they had information for us. We never knew when or how new information would arrive, but it kept us connected to the war effort on the outside.

All the Germans ever told us was how efficient they were in achieving their victories. Their strict routines were starting to become unpredictable though, and small groups of soldiers were standing around camp having discussions about the end of the war. We would listen to their comments to gage the war's progress. We were aware of how they tried to keep the truth from us, but it was clear from their grim faces that not all of them believed the propaganda they spoke about.

Nazi authority over the Polish people was going to end; it was simply a matter of time. That thought filled me with enough hope to resolutely choose life every day. It was only because of that choice that I could endure the most dismal situations, day after day. The simple truth was, the soldiers didn't see our humanity, but that fact didn't mean I was unaware of it. Had they been persuaded into believing that the hatred they implemented for the sake of their leader was really going to lead to a pure race?

I kept hoping that maybe a small realization was starting to awaken in them. Like a seedling's first fragile leaves, growing bigger in time, awareness might be starting to creep into their minds, softening their hearts, just a bit. I wondered what they thought about their "Führer" now. They did like to put on a good show, make everything look smart, even if the foundation was starting to crumble.

The beautification project was getting close to being finished – at least on the outside. It reminded me of the Bible's words about whitewashing a tomb to make it appear clean and bright, but the inside was still filled with death and decay. The German commander was determined to show the delegation that we were a model school. Would the visitors look beyond the white-washing?

We still needed to learn songs and receive our jobs for the stork festival. I wondered about the music and the food for the festival. I kept thinking about the pickles and the *pirogues* – unleavened dough filled with mashed potatoes, cabbage, onions and meat. They were delicious, but took quite a bit of time to make. I watched my grandmother and mama make them many times. My grandmother grew the cucumbers that my mama turned into the best pickles. They were some of my favorite foods. I also wondered where they would find the musicians. I was sure they had a plan for everything. Even though it was all a hoax to trick the Red Cross delegates, it was still exciting to smell the food, hear the singing and see something other than the dreary camp we found ourselves entombed in. My senses were starved for some kind of normal display of life, even if it was only for a short time and just pretend.

Stacks of fresh straw mattresses were piled outside each barrack. We weren't allowed to touch them and I suppose the Germans would only put them in our bunks for the day of the Red Cross visit. Our bodies would never come in contact with them. Knowing the Germans, they would remove them quickly from the bunk-beds after the visiting delegates left the camp.

One area of camp life was definitely improving for us specifically – the food. For the past two days we actually received food three times during the day instead of only twice. There were sausages, potatoes and other vegetables in our soup, and it was in a thick milky broth instead of water. We also got milk every morning and night. It had been years since I'd tasted milk, and I'd truly forgotten how delicious it was. I wondered how they would hide our skinny, skeleton-like bodies, but at least for a week or so we would have more food. Some of the children were looking for places to hide some of their food. They didn't trust that the Germans would continue to feed us like this after the Red Cross visit. I knew better than to hide food in my bunk. If the guards found it, I would receive a beating.

All of the normal food was having an unanticipated reaction on the digestive systems of the children who had been here the longest, including me. It seems the richness was too much for our starved bodies and stomachs. It was torture to be so hungry, and then immediately after eating, to find that we had to quickly run for the outhouse. The food was coming back up for many of us, as our shrunken stomachs refused to make room for unaccustomed food. Anna began to worry about me, but I assured her that I'd be fine after the representatives' visit. I was confident that once we resumed our old eating habits my stomach would return to normal.

Anna, as well as some of the newer, younger children had started going to classes in the new camp school. The older inmates still worked in the factories and fields. The sign above the Litzmannstadt Labor Camp had been changed to "Litzmannstadt School." I tried to gently warn Anna that the classroom situation was probably only temporary. She seemed to understand her part in the deception the Nazis were staging for the representatives. I hoped she wasn't thinking about speaking with any of the delegates, and filling them in on the details of the real conditions that existed in this miserable place. I could see how she would be tempted to do that, but such a bold move would only jeopardize her safety and possibly her life.

The Nazi commander was famous for making an example out of a child who had misbehaved in some way. Public beating or sending the offender to another camp was usually the way he handled such defiance. Both types of punishment had lasting effects on those of us who were forced to witness it. The Nazis took such perverse pleasure in their ability to torture children. I could close my eyes during such times, but was forbidden to cover my ears. Hearing those sounds was agony for the children forced to bear witness to the brutality. A mass of fear and disgust

packed the hearts of the children, filling the juveniles in atten-
dance with resolve to survive. It was proof that sometimes, fear
and anger can be a good motivator.

I was very curious about what they did all day in school. I
asked Anna about her time in the classroom.

"What's it like, Anna? Is it like a real school?"

She shrugged, then said, "I can't speak their language, but I do
understand most of it."

"So what do you do?"

"I watch the other children and do whatever I see them do. It
seems kind of dull, but I like it better than working in the kitchen
or factory. Some of the kids told me the math questions were
dumb."

"What do you mean, Anna?"

"I don't know, you should ask Berta."

"Ok, if I get a chance, I will."

"You have a good day and don't get in any trouble today, ok?"

"Ok, Ewa, I won't. I'll see you tonight." Anna headed off to
school.

I wondered how long the school would continue after the Red
Cross visit. I was confident it would end immediately after the
delegates left. I was bothered by Anna's remark about the math
questions. What could she have meant by that remark? Was this
school another deliberate attempt of the Nazis to Germanize the
children? We'd already lost that battle, that's why we were here.

I needed to calm myself down; we had no rights, or claims to
anything here. Even if it was only temporary, at least Anna got a
break from the mindless, difficult labor inflicted upon us. I
cautioned myself to focus on what I needed to do this morning,
which was to get my work assignment for the day.

I was hopeful that I would get another chance to look for the
storks while working outside. I must be working on straw shoes
today. Then suddenly, I realized I'd been daydreaming again.
Everyone was walking away and assembling into their work

groups but I hadn't heard my name called for any group. I hoped that didn't mean I was on camp clean-up. I couldn't bear the feelings I got when cleaning around the sick children shivering in their bunks, burning up with fever, too sick to eat or make it outside before losing the contents of their stomachs. Camp life was too harsh for many of the children; homesick, starved, cold, lonely, so many succumbed to illness. It was a known fact that if you went to the camp doctor you probably wouldn't come back, so most kids tried to avoid appearing ill. I always forced myself to attend roll call and receive a job assignment, no matter how ill I felt. Now, I had Anna to consider as well as myself.

Then I saw the young soldier I'd spoken with the day I'd gotten Anna out of the barracks and away from the dog. He approached me with his dog and an older man. I searched my brain for some kind of explanation. *Was I in trouble? Would I be the next example of public discipline? What could this possibly mean?* I reminded myself to breathe and stay calm even though my legs were betraying me and starting to shake.

"Ewa, right?"

I nodded my head.

"We have a special job for you today."

"Something we think you deserve, and will be very good at performing."

Experience had taught me that changes in a place like this were usually bad. This was a change I hadn't anticipated. I was familiar with the different jobs we did here. I'd been doing them for years. Perhaps this had to do with the beautification program though.

I didn't know what to think. I was slightly relieved about the "special job" they had for me, even though my heart sank with disappointment because once again this meant I'd have to wait at least one more day before looking for the storks. I found myself being silently escorted by two large, uniformed men. They walked with ram rod stiffness, spotless uniforms, and boots shining to perfection; one in front of me and one behind me, taking long steps making it difficult for me to keep up with them. I hoped we weren't going very far because I didn't know how long I could continue this pace. I was used to traveling to job sites in groups of children; guards slowing slightly to accommodate the steps of smaller feet in the group. The fact that I was by myself, being escorted by two soldiers made me feel uneasy, but it was too late. If I tried to escape I'd be shot. The fear I felt was like a shiny necklace hanging around my neck for all to see. Fortunately, it didn't take long to arrive at our destination.

Circling slowly, climbing higher, white wings gleaming in the sun.

Floating, gliding on the airstreams, storks and Poland, home as one.

The storks make their long migration from southern Africa back to Poland. Along the way, they stop in Sudan in northern Africa. The availability of locusts in Africa provides them the nourishment they need for their winter survival and spring departure. The journey takes them between 20 and 30 days. During their arduous migration, they avoid the Black Sea and the Mediterranean Sea by crossing the Bosporus Strait in Istanbul, Turkey. They are reluctant to fly across large bodies of water because they like to glide, and thermal air currents are not found over water.

The route they've traveled for centuries has remained fixed because of the geographical location of the seas. Storks rely on soaring during migration. Storks glide on convection thermals from high altitudes of 480 to 1600 meters.

Turkey remained neutral until February of 1945 when it declared war against Germany.

For the most part, the storks continue their yearly migrations unimpeded by war.

Chapter 10

Gratitude

Both parents bring food to the nest until the young fledge is eight to nine weeks of age.

The word deserve can mean to triumph, merit or succeed. You may have an opportunity to triumph at something, receive merit for an accomplishment, or succeed at acquiring what you deserve. The Nazis tried to justify taking a country they didn't deserve. Being triumphant doesn't necessarily mean you deserve what you've taken. I felt the Nazis didn't deserve our country. They could not take our country's soul by destroying its body. I knew the storks understood that instinctively because of what they gave Poland, not by what they took. Our holidays, culture, traditions and festivals were built around these birds. Our seasons were noted by their migration patterns. Our farms flourished because they helped keep the agricultural ecosystems in check by eating grasshoppers, insects and mice. A long relationship, built on certainty and trust, existed between the birds and the people.

* * *

The soldiers told me I deserved this job, but there was no trust or certainty. I searched my memory for the expression on the young guard's face. There must be some clue about the special job they had in store for me; something I would be good at. Over the years I'd tried to learn what the soldiers' different expressions meant. Like books in a library, some of the guards were easier to read than others. I'd learned that if a soldier sounded strict and stern, yet his eyes revealed sadness or softness, I would probably be safe. That phrasing, "deserve," rolled around in my head as I tried to attach it to something I could understand.

I couldn't read this man's face though, and the older one wouldn't make eye contact with me, which was never a good sign. His face was like stone, cold and hard, unaffected. A shiver went down my spine and I told myself to breathe – then I heard the familiar swishing sound of the storks' large wings.

I paused and looked up just as one flew over and quickly disappeared from view, hidden by the rows and rows of barracks. It was so beautiful in the morning light of early spring. Its white feathers looked far whiter than I ever remembered them, and the early morning sunlight made its shadowed parts appear purple. The dark wing tips looked beautiful against the white feathers. I knew where it was headed, to the barns and churches just beyond the camp, to the same nest that it had used year after year.

Our culture was so enchanted by our beloved *bociek* that we had folk sayings about them.

"If storks arrive on St. Joseph's Day, the snows will soon melt away. If they arrive on Annunciation Day, a stork will be in its nest to stay, and if they arrive on St. Wojciech's Day, the stork an egg will lay."

We even had a saying for when the stork leaves Poland and heads back to Africa. "On St. Bartholomew's Day, the stork prepares to be on its way."

The male stork is the first to arrive. His job is to fix and repair the nest and make sure it will hold up for the new family that will be arriving soon. The nests are constructed of branches and sticks and lined with grasses, twigs, and anything the stork can find to line it with. The male also needs to locate the food sources in the area. Storks are carnivores. They dine on frogs, fish, insects, small rodents, lizards, and worms. The female arrives a few days later. The female usually lays three to five eggs, and both parents help keep the eggs warm for a month until they hatch.

Every town in Poland celebrates the arrival of the storks. Even though I was walking forward into a situation that was unfamiliar, I knew I would be alright. I'd seen a stork, the first stork of spring, so a blessing and a measure of good luck was upon my head now. A pang of longing touched my heart as my grandfather's face slid into my memory. I was thanking grandpa in my mind when we abruptly stopped.

The sound of gates being unlocked and opened brought me back to reality. I was ushered into an area that looked like a prisoner compound with extra rows of fencing. I had never seen this part of the camp before. Inmates were only allowed in certain areas of the camp. This place was behind so many rows of wire fencing and buildings that it had definitely been off limits, and had escaped my awareness. It was farther away from the barracks that housed the children and the regular guards. The older man called out some orders in German. A door at the end of the building immediately opened and several young recruits, expressions locked in attentiveness, ran out of the building with what looked like young German Shepherd dogs, a few years old. I was stunned. Not only were the dogs young but the soldiers handling them appeared to be quite young also. I had no idea that so many dog teams were housed here.

I'd only seen the same two dogs in our barrack day in and day out. I'd seen very few other canines, and only at a distance while they were on sentry duty, or accompanying us to and from our work sites. The officer informed the soldiers that I would be tending their dogs. He commanded the dog handlers to walk them to their houses and release them. The dogs were very obedient and lay calmly in their houses.

I often felt sorry for the dogs that had sentry duty. It was nothing like watching the herding work our dogs performed. Our German Shepherds looked energized, like they were having fun. These sentry dogs looked bored, like their handlers; like I felt when working in the factory. My curiosity was getting to me. *What was I doing here? What could they possibly want from me?* I figured they wanted me to clean their kennels, but it didn't make sense that they wanted me to interact with the dogs. Most animals bonded with their caretakers, especially dogs. A German Shepherd by nature is wary of strangers, but once they accept the stranger, they are friends for life. These dogs are very social and love human companionship. They are playful as well as fierce protectors. I didn't think they wanted their dogs to bond with me, though. Did they even know what they were risking?

This situation presented itself with such an unusual set of circumstances. I loved dogs but was terrified of the soldiers. When I'd rescued Anna in the barracks I hadn't had time to think about what I was doing, but now I was confronted with a new job involving soldiers and dogs. If I interacted with the dogs, would they sense the fear I felt for their handlers? I wasn't sure what they wanted from me so I reminded myself to act cautiously.

The older man spoke in German to the soldiers, telling them that I would be responsible for cleaning the kennels, cleaning the dogs and caring for them, but I was not to feed them. The young men still had that duty. I wondered about my new responsibilities. Would the dogs listen to me? Would they respond to what I expected of them? What would the soldiers think if they saw their dogs interacting with a Polish girl? After all, we were a people that their country's leader viewed as inferior and worthy of destruction. This camp was full of children that hadn't qualified for the Germanization process. We were actually lower in their eyes than the dogs.

It had been so many years since I'd handled a dog. I wondered if I was up to the task. Was it even possible for me to remember everything my papa and grandfather had taught me about caring for dogs? It felt like a lifetime ago since I'd helped on our farm. I had never cared for a dog used in sentry duty before, only herding dogs. Even though I could speak German fluently, I secretly cautioned myself to measure my words carefully when speaking to the dogs. I reminded myself not to become too comfortable with this job. Dogs could usually be trusted once you knew them, but German soldiers never could. I knew if I slipped up and spoke Polish I would be beaten if overheard by a soldier.

One thing about this job quickened the pace of my heart. Just a few yards beyond the kennel fence was a forest. A slight breeze carried the earthy, sweet scent of trees to my nose. I could smell the Christmassy scent of the Norway spruce. I could actually hear the wind whispering through the tops of the trees, a sound I'd longed for since arriving here. I eyed the clouds moving over the trees. Heavy and dark, they looked as if rain was about to spill out of them like a bucket dumping water. The tree branches bent and swayed in the wind as if taunting me to come play. I closed my eyes and took a big deep breath; sighing, I opened my eyes. You could say I was in my element…well, almost.

The young sentry, rigid with soldier-like posture, brought me back to the task at hand. He was quickly explaining all the details of the job he wanted me to perform. I was having trouble listening because I couldn't get my mind off the forest that stood only a few yards away. I was here to clean the kennel, replace the straw in the dog houses, give them fresh water, clean the water trough, groom and exercise the dogs. He showed me where the tools and supplies were kept. I was reminded not to feed the dogs. That job was still the responsibility of the soldiers.

"Ewa, do you have any questions?"

I shook my head back and forth.

"Are you sure?"

"Yes, I'm sure."

"Ok, I'll leave you to the job, then. I will come back later and check on you."

He grabbed my chin with his gloved hand and squeezed it between his fingers and thumb, using vice-like pressure, forcing me to look at him.

His eyes were bluish gray. With a low, menacing growl he spit out his warning.

"You will keep this job if you strictly obey. Are we clear on that?"

"Yes," I replied as water leaked out of the rims of my eyes.

My face felt bruised where the soldier's intimidating grip had pinched it. Opening my mouth and stretching my jaw relieved some of the soreness he'd left behind. The marks, if visible, would leave in time. The memory, though, would last a lifetime.

The gate slammed shut, the chains were locked and he quickly left. Breathing a sigh of relief, I looked around. I stood in the middle of an elongated enclosure. Looking from one end of the kennel to the other, the dog houses lined one side of the rectangular area. There was a lengthy trough half full of water that needed to be cleaned and changed. Green scum floated on the top reminding me of our pond back home. Most of the dogs were lying in their houses, eyeing me. I knew to move slowly while acting confident and calm. I began to hum as I moved toward the row of crate-like houses.

I walked over to the closest dog house. I stood about five feet away and held out my hand so the dog could sniff it. She timidly left her house, approaching me cautiously as I spoke to her in a low, soothing voice, assuring her that I wasn't there to hurt her. I was going to have to work for this dog's trust. She was very shy, almost to the point of cowering. After letting her sniff my hand, she allowed me to pet her gently. I kept talking in a serene voice. She seemed stressed; she was panting heavily, and I wanted her to know I wouldn't hurt her. I wondered how long she'd been in this camp. She looked young even though she was a good size. After she became comfortable with me, in a few days, I would look at her teeth and see if I could get an idea of her age. I looked at her collar. Her name was Mitzi.

"Hi Mitzi, how are you today? My name is Ewa."

She cocked her head to the side and looked at me calmly, wagging her tail slightly. Her panting slowed down… good, one dog down, fifteen more to go. Perhaps some of the dogs would be more trusting than Mitzi. It was going to take time to get to know them individually. I started thinking about how long I would be doing this job. I was sure it would be longer than just today, after all, the Red Cross visit was quickly approaching. Wouldn't the Commander want the kennel as well as the dogs to look as good as the rest of the camp? I hoped I could work here until liberation. I recalled the guard's warning about keeping the job. I looked at the forest.

"I'll be there soon," I whispered. "They can't keep me away forever."

The tree branches bowed in the breeze, acknowledging my remark.

Fear no longer hung like a shiny necklace from my neck. It began to be replaced with calmness and familiarity. I could do this job with my eyes closed. There wasn't a Nazi standing over me screaming "work faster." There was only me, and the dogs, and the forest just outside the fence. Not only was I outside where I could look for storks, I was working with dogs, by myself, with a beautiful green forest a few yards away. *How was this possible?* I started working. This was a job I enjoyed.

"Thank you," I whispered.

Gratitude filled my heart as papa's face filled my mind.

Chapter 11

Judgment

The storks eat a wide variety of prey items including insects, frogs, toads, fish, rodents, snakes, lizards, earthworms, and other prey found on the ground.

Judgment is an interesting word. It can cause someone to exercise restraint, control or fear. The strength in a balanced judgment is that it can result in justice, balance, and fairness.

My father never sold a dog to a farmer until he'd watched him work his sheep. He wanted to match up the personality traits of the dogs and the farmers so they would become a successful team. Successful teams meant farmers would return to him for more dogs. I hadn't realized how many of his training techniques had rubbed off on me. It seemed natural for me to notice the personalities and interactions of the dogs and handlers. The timid dogs needed someone more patient and kind. It seemed as though these teams hadn't been properly matched, but that wasn't my concern. I was only here to clean the kennel and tend the dogs. The less the Germans knew about my abilities the better. I liked working with the dogs because it took me back to a better time in my life. It seemed like a lifetime ago – an era before the war. When I was working in the dog kennel, at least for a little while each day, I could pretend I was back on our farm.

I preferred watching my papa put the dogs through their training exercises instead of attending school. School, so completely different from our land and the forest, was not my favorite place to be. School was so measured, regulated, controlled, while the forest was magical with its endless variety and curiosities. I felt so alive in the forest and so restricted in school.

Those thoughts and memories hadn't visited me in a long time. I'm glad they returned; like snowflakes falling slowly from the sky, piling up in a mound, waiting for me to dig in and lessen the feelings of seclusion and sadness in my heart. I hated the thought I was helping Germany, but every job in the camp was supporting Germany in some way. I felt selfish because I had a job I actually liked. There was so much misery here. How was it possible that I took pleasure in anything? Somehow, working with the dogs made me feel human again. Until now, feelings of joy and love rarely came to me during daylight. Usually, happiness only visited in my dreams at night. Often I would daydream to feel safe; any feelings other than the constant loneliness and fear I felt were unexpected and wonderful. Somehow my memories sustained me even though I was finding less and less time to daydream.

After years of living here I was nothing more than a skeleton, doing physical labor and following strict orders. Now, working with the dogs I could willingly slip into my memories and feel some comfort if only for a limited time each day. Maybe it was simply the fact that the dogs had no choice in the matter either. I felt almost as much compassion for them as I did for the children that were in the camp. I knew that when the war ended the dogs would possibly be destroyed. It would be difficult but not impossible to retrain them for something other than sentry duty. What would happen to the children? Even though they wouldn't face the same outcome as the dogs, would they have homes and families to return to? Would they be able to resume their lives or would they be forever changed and unable to take up where their previous lives had ended? What would life after the camp and barbed wire fence hold for them – justice, balance, fairness?

How devastated would they be with their country, their culture and possibly many family members gone? These questions were not easily answered because there were too many possibilities. Other questions came to mind. Would Poland ever recover? How would family members be reunited? It tired me to think so about the future, and not have answers to these really significant questions.

I wanted justice for myself as well as my country. I longed for someone to step in and hold the Nazis accountable for their actions. I would just have to trust that everything would come full circle, like the seasons of the year and the habits of the storks. Life as we once knew it would return, changed, but familiar. Maybe that's why God gave us nature, so we would remember that spring follows winter and storms don't last forever.

* * *

For now I needed to clean and put fresh straw in the dog kennels. As I replaced old straw I couldn't help wishing we were as fortunate. We slept on rough boards with thin, lice-infested, straw mats and rags for blankets, huddling together for warmth while these dogs had plenty of room with clean, fresh straw that smelled so earthy. It looked as though it was very comfortable to lie down on. I found myself tempted to crawl into one of the dog houses and take a nap. The thought of curling up in the late morning sun on fresh straw with a warm, furry dog was so tempting, if only for a minute, but did I dare take such a chance? If I was caught, I would lose my job and probably be beaten. I looked at all the dogs. This was one job I wanted to keep.

I still needed to bring fresh water, haul out all the waste to the dump pit, and brush each dog. I needed to pace myself. I continued going down the line letting each dog smell my hand and gradually feel comfortable with me. It would take some time for them to trust me, and feel secure with me.

After loading the waste, I stepped outside the gate pulling the heavy wagon behind me. I stopped for a second to catch my breath. Going outside the camp fence alone felt so odd. I'd never been out by myself before. I knew I was being watched by the lookout guard, but it still felt like I was on my own. I was so tempted to walk into the forest. It was only a few yards from the dumping pit. Trees reached out their boughs encouraging me to enter their shade and shelter. Chills went down my spine at the very thought of trying to venture out. Even if I was successful in getting away undetected, what would I do on my own in the forest and how would I get back home? I wasn't even sure how far this forest reached; perhaps it was only a narrow patch of trees. I had no plan, and I couldn't afford to be impulsive about this. I believed liberation was coming, possibly within the next few weeks or months. Besides that, I still had Anna to think about. What would happen to her if I didn't look out for her? I cautioned myself to forget any thought of escape and just finish my work. I could feel the lookout's steady gaze on my back. It was almost as if he'd read my thoughts. His eyes burned a hole in my back as I finished emptying the wooden wagon of used straw and dog waste. I headed back to the gate under the suspicious glare of the guard. I still needed to brush and exercise the dogs, as well as haul water from the pump to fill the trough. That would take quite a while, one bucket at a time. Nothing was easy or convenient here; everything was done in the simplest way possible, which only made more work for us.

I was anxious to return to the other side of the compound, and find out what everyone had seen or heard today while working on the cleanup program. Usually we were too exhausted to talk at night. However, the new look of the camp along with the extra meal and milk had given us more energy and we often whispered about anything we'd heard during the day, before drifting off to sleep. It was amazing to watch the girls in my barrack have more energy and become excited at the prospect of the war ending soon. I wasn't the only one assigned to a new job. Many of us were given jobs we had never performed before. Along with the increased food, the new jobs put an end to the monotonous routines we lived by and helped us forge ahead even though our future was unpredictable.

Despite the fact that I had only been working in the dog kennel for a few hours, I knew all of the dogs by name. I also noticed which ones were more dominant and which ones were timid. I checked their ears to determine which ones needed cleaning to keep them free of mites. I also checked their feet for injured pads. Sometimes the dogs' feet would become sore and tender if they'd walked on a lot of cement or rocks, much like people trying to walk on blistered feet. After this last inspection I still needed to brush them, but I had to make sure I didn't run out of time.

I started to become especially attached to one male in particular. He reminded me so much of Basil. He had the same calm, intelligent demeanor as Basil. His size was even similar, though his markings weren't. He had one ear tip that flopped over slightly and refused to stand at attention like most German Shepherds' ears. He was the first one to take an interest in me. He followed me wherever I was working in the kennel, and when I left to haul water or dump waste he sat attentively by the gate, as if he was patiently awaiting my return.

His name was Hardy, and although I knew it would not be a benefit for either of us to bond, I could not help myself. German Shepherds are genuinely loyal dogs and extremely intelligent. If he showed any favoritism towards me while on sentry duty it could cost one or both of us our lives. His behaviors, however, drew me irresistibly to him. He reminded me so much of Basil, I couldn't keep myself from becoming captivated. His eagerness to engage me in play, his attentiveness and interest in me held me captive and made me feel special. Once again, I longed to feel the warmth and love of what I'd left behind, my family, home and Basil. Despite my concerns about connecting to Hardy, I became very attached to him. Working with him brought back emotions I had not felt for a long time. These weren't feelings based on memory; these were brought on by interacting with my physical world. A world that until now, I had loathed and tried to avoid as much as possible.

I was showing restraint in so many areas of my life – daily routines, following orders – but now those walls were crashing down, and I was frightened. If an aspect of judgment is showing restraint, I was doing the opposite where Hardy and Anna were concerned. I was so captivated by them. This was just the right mix of companionship, devotion and attraction; giving me back some of what I'd left in Kostrzyn, and I couldn't walk away. I knew if it came down to choosing them or walking away...I would choose them. Anna told me very little about her family. I didn't know if she had a family to return to. Hardy would be abandoned, shot or retrained. I couldn't leave either of them to an unknown fate. When I left this camp, it wouldn't be by myself.

Chapter 12

Connection

Storks are considered to be silent birds, but white storks throw their heads back and clatter their upper and lower bills together rapidly, making a loud rattle.

Several days passed with the same work schedule. Anna attended school every day while I worked in the kennels. I had lived with various degrees of fear for the past few years. Now I was trying to balance the fear I felt with the joy I felt over the connection I was developing with Hardy. How could I possibly keep from drawing close to him? He reminded me of everything I had left behind, everything I loved and missed. Just being around him made my heart feel lighter, and during off-duty times I found myself thinking of him more and more, wondering if he was waiting at the gate for me. I could not let myself become attached to the kids here, because our lives were extremely fleeting. I recalled the girl from the factory, tossed into the transport truck like a chunk of wood being tossed on a fire. We couldn't count on being here from one day to the next. The Germans could ship us off to an extermination camp, or another labor camp, at any time. I'd already broken an unspoken rule by helping Anna. Now, I felt very protective of her and made sure to show her every day how special she was. Like a baby bird working to emerge from its shell, she was finally starting to scratch at the protective scab she was in. She was talking a bit more and taking an interest in finding out about my day. I started seeing signs of the real Anna seep out. She would slowly dole out a memory from happier times, or share her hope for the future. Even though she was terrified of dogs she asked about Hardy and his new antics.

The dogs were treated better than the Polish children and I felt I could count on them being here until the end of the war, even if there was no guarantee that I would still be here. I silently reminded myself of how long it took me to get over Basil. Did I have it in me to go through that kind of grief again if something should happen to Hardy? I wondered who his handler was, and if he cared for Hardy as much as I did. Did he notice how intelligent Hardy was and how eager he was to please?

I started scrubbing down the kennel. Afterwards, I threw buckets of water to wash away the soap. I replaced all the straw bedding with clean, fresh straw. I scrubbed down the water trough and filled it to the top with clean water. It sparkled when I was finished. I brushed the few dogs who weren't working and hauled all of the waste outside the camp to the rubbish pit. My arms felt heavy from all the lifting and hauling. Suddenly, I was so fatigued and I noticed my hunger for the first time since the morning.

After a long day of cleaning I felt exhausted and wanted to go to sleep. My grandmother's lullaby played in my mind.

"*Dobrej nocy, I sza, do bialego spij dnia. Spij dziecino, oczka zmruz, Spij do wschodu rannych zorz.*"

"Goodnight and hush, sleep 'till the morning comes. Sleep my baby, close your eyes, Sleep 'till the dawn will shine."

I skipped dinner and went straight to my bunk. Anna couldn't hide the worry on her face. I reassured her that I was just tired, not sick. When Anna came to the bunk I softly sang the lullaby that my grandmother used to sing to me. I said a quick prayer, asking for deliverance from our situation. I had Anna by my side. I pulled the rags we used for warmth up over us. The weather was definitely getting warmer and we weren't freezing all the time, but the nights were still cooling down quite a bit and we needed each other for warmth. It's so hard to feel warm when you don't have any fat on your body. Shivering seemed to be a common reaction to any temperature other than hot weather. I took some comfort in the fact that soon the hot weather and temperatures would be here.

I pictured my family in my mind, saying good night to each one individually. It felt like they were in the next room and not miles and miles away from me.

A heavy quiet hung over the barrack like an old woolen winter coat. I could hear the steady breathing of the girls around me. I was so tired that even the wooden bunk felt comfortable. My work with the dogs was satisfying but tiring. I'd quickly learned here that normal everyday desires, like taking a nap or going to the bathroom, or eating a snack, or getting a drink of fresh, cool water without permission were strictly forbidden. It dawned on me how regimented my life had become. Almost every normal freedom I'd taken for granted was not something I could even consider or act on now. I missed those small freedoms tremendously.

One of the drawbacks to more daylight and warmer weather meant the Germans could keep us working longer hours. It seemed like the work was endless. We were never in a hurry to finish a job because they always came up with another one. If the guards could tell we were stalling and taking too long to complete a task, the yelling and hitting would encourage us to speed it up. The threat of missing a meal seemed to have the biggest impact on us, though.

With any luck at all we'd be out of this camp soon. The Polish underground assured us that the war was close to ending. Germany was being pushed back on all fronts. It seemed possible that they were close to the point of collapse. We also had the Red Cross visit to look forward to. Perhaps the delegates could inform us about an end to the war, or how the end would be handled when it finally arrived. How would we be transported home?

I didn't know, however, if we'd be permitted to speak with them. The Germans, on the other hand, were acting more and more confident every day. Usually we only had to listen to the commander's crazy speeches about Germany's greatness once a month. Now, however, it seemed like we were hearing these speeches weekly. It reminded me of a dog that is cornered, bares its teeth and growls out of fear.

We'd already heard, months ago, that the Soviets had turned on Germany. Germany broke the pact with Russia in June of 1941. The Soviets had helped in the destruction of our country but now they were no longer allies with Germany. Until now, the Polish Resistance had been involved in sabotage, reprisal and diversion tactics against the Germans. The main goal was to weaken their potential and lower their morale. Factory, farm and railroad workers all found ways to delay and damage machinery that supported Germany's economic value and war economy. Polish laborers functioned under the motto, "As little, as late and as slow as possible." Sabotage activities of average Polish citizens were so all-encompassing that it was viewed as effective as several divisions fighting on the front. Direct contact with the Germans, however, was side-stepped because it resulted in vicious punishments. Perhaps the end of the war was closer than we realized, but for now, I just needed sleep.

Anna cuddled up next to me on our narrow bunk. My concern for her was always on my mind. She'd been more tired than usual lately even though we were getting more food. I blamed the hunger – always the gnawing, grinding, empty feeling of not having enough food. The hunger was like a herding dog, tenacious, constant, never giving up. I had to find a way to sneak some dog food to her, but how? I didn't want Anna to go see the camp doctor so I had to find a way to strengthen her. Maybe my dreams would show me how to help her. I closed my heavy eyelids, sinking into the luxury of sleep. The last thing I remember was a childhood song playing in my head. I didn't wake until I heard the soldiers yelling and the air raid sirens going off.

Rags flying, arms and legs flailing like windmills, we leaped off our beds. There was no place for us to go except under the stacked wooden bunks. Quickly and quietly we crammed ourselves under the lowest bed. We didn't dare leave the barrack. The air raid shelters spaced at regular intervals around the perimeter of the camp were for the soldiers only. They were close to the barracks and open enough for the guards to see us and shoot us if we tried to leave the building. We didn't utter a sound; we just listened. We could hear the loud blasts of bombs hitting targets somewhere outside the camp. Occasionally, we felt the floor shake from the concussion of a bomb, but the most terrifying thing was the sound of it all, and the feeling of helplessness. I said a quick prayer asking that all the prisoners' barracks be spared. I hoped Hardy was safe.

I closed my eyes tightly and wrapped my arms around Anna, saying, "It will be over soon, Anna, don't cry."

Anna was terrified and cried silently, sobs shaking her body.

"Someday this will all be over, Anna, we'll be ok and this will be a distant memory to us."

What else could I say? How do you tell a terrified person not to be afraid, especially when she had every right to be frightened? The night air raids were coming more frequently. How did they know which areas to bomb and which to avoid? I often wondered if our rescuers knew we were down here. For now, all I could offer her was a strong embrace and soothing words. I silently prayed that this would pass quickly. No matter how uncomfortable my bed was, at least it was better than the floor. Was it the chill of the spring night air, or the circumstance of being bombed that caused me to shiver? I could not lie here much longer, and my back was starting to ache. The thin straw mats that lined our bunks weren't much, but they did offer padding against the wood we laid our bodies on. I think we might have been as safe in our beds as under them, but I didn't want to risk getting caught disobeying.

Chapter 13

Mercy

As the baby birds prepare for their first flight, they practice by jumping up from the ground floor of the nest, and then take small flights near the nest.

Mercy is showing affection, altruism, and compassion. I'm not sure if it's harder showing emotions you don't feel, or harder hiding what you shouldn't feel. Navigating through these feelings was confusing even as some things were becoming very clear. I needed to hide my feelings of affection for Anna and Hardy, but only when guards were present or watching. I needed to show the guards respect even though I felt contempt for them. It was a slippery slope for me. I had to pay attention to my feelings all the time, and recognize when to ignore them and when to act on them.

* * *

Anna and I jumped up quickly and folded our ragged blankets and placed them on the end of our bunk the minute we heard the morning siren. I was so tired last night that I didn't remember climbing back into bed after the air raid. We grabbed our metal cups and headed for the soup line. Word quickly spread down the line that we had potatoes and some sausage in our soup again this morning! This would be good for us, especially Anna. We were starting to get potatoes, vegetables and some meat a bit more often because of the Red Cross visit. It didn't make sense to me though, because potatoes were only just now being planted, not harvested. After they filled our cups I noticed it was not the usual potato peels, but actual potatoes. In the past, only the soldiers received the potatoes in their soup, along with other vegetables and meat.

Grateful for the hearty soup, we grabbed our bread and headed to the sun to sit and eat. We only had a short time to eat and use the bathroom before roll call and job assignments began. Today the weather was warm and sunny – a perfect spring day. Surely I would see another stork today. I recalled how the villages used to celebrate spring's arrival. Actually, the stork celebrations were more of a combination between the end of Lent and the beginning of Easter celebration. Spring was always a busy time on our farm. There were certain routines you could count on season after season, year after year, much like the church traditions and the nature of the storks. There were all kinds of baby animals being born, seeds and crops to plant, spring cleaning in the house and barn. It was a very hectic time of year and one of my favorite seasons. I longed for the realization of rebirth that nature brought in the springtime.

Anna was unusually quiet even after eating the hearty soup.

"Anna, are you ok?"

She only nodded yes. She had a far-away look in her eyes and a faint smile on her face. I knew she was thinking about something or someone from a happier time.

"Anna, there's something I need to tell you but you must promise me that you won't breathe a word of it to anyone...you promise?"

She nodded again and lifted her tired eyes to look at me.

"Yesterday, when I was finished taking care of the dogs and getting ready to leave the kennels, I overheard a soldier speaking to another soldier about planning an escape because the end of the war was coming and Germany was losing! You've got to promise me, Anna, that you won't give up, promise me!"

Anna shook her head slowly up and down as if contemplating was using too much energy. I put my hand on her shoulder to reassure her; wincing at the frailty of what I felt.

Even with the extra soup and milk, the years of war had taken their toll on Anna's health. It wasn't just here that we were denied food. It was all over Poland, and all over Europe. People were starving everywhere. Everyone, except the German soldiers; they individually received more food in one day than a Polish child received in one week. Pursuing genocide by malnutrition was exactly what Hermann Goering, in charge of national defense, had in mind when he openly declared, "If anyone goes hungry, it certainly would not be the Germans." This belief was consistent with the Nazi view that the Poles were racially inferior and needed less food. When I came to this camp, most of the children arrived here looking thin but somewhat healthy. I noticed as the war progressed, more and more of the children arrived starved, and already suffering from malnutrition. Anna was skin and bones. She desperately needed food. I had to get her some.

"Anna, I'll sneak you some food today, just please, don't give up."

She looked at me again, with sadness and resignation in her eyes.

"Come on, we must use the bathroom before roll call." I helped her up and placed our cups in the wash tub near the camp kitchen.

I wondered if the lessons she was learning in the new school were upsetting her. As I waited in line to use the bathroom, I asked Berta if she knew anything about the lessons in the school. I knew she had gone through some schooling under the Germanization program.

Berta looked around, then pulled a piece of paper out of her pocket. It was from the math book. She showed me one of the math questions. *"A bomber aircraft on takeoff carries 12 dozen bombs, each weighing 10 kilos. The aircraft takes off for Warsaw. It bombs the town, killing as many Poles as possible. On takeoff with all bombs on board and a fuel tank containing 100 kilos of fuel, the aircraft weighed about 8 tons. When it returns from the crusade, there are still 230 kilos left. What is the weight of the aircraft when empty?"*

She also told me that all of the questions in their math books promoted Nazi beliefs. No wonder Anna felt so upset after listening to those questions. It would be like taking a bath in a mud puddle and expecting to come out clean. Even children recognize humiliation and disrespect. There's a place in your soul that is bruised by it.

We took our places in formation, sun hitting our backs, listening to the camp commander drone on about the camp rules and the great importance of doing our best for Germany. The Red Cross visit must be getting close, but we still hadn't received instructions for the stork festival or the songs we were supposed to perform. Even though the sun was warm on my back I could see Anna shivering. She was so skinny it scared me. Worry paid a visit to my stomach, causing a hunger-like twinge to tie it in knots. I said a quick prayer that she would survive until liberation. It had to be soon, but would it be soon enough?

I already knew my work assignment for the day, but stayed near Anna until she got hers. Good, she was assigned to the camp kitchen, where she would peel potatoes and help prepare soup.

"Anna, try to eat some potato peels today, ok? But don't get caught!"

I was so glad she was getting a break from school today; besides, she would have an opportunity to steal some food. I squeezed Anna's hand. I wanted to hug her and protect her. She smiled and slowly headed in the direction of the camp kitchen, head down, shoulders rounded, with the posture of an old woman.

"Please God, help Anna today."

The soldier escorting me to the kennels had arrived. I took a deep breath, my eyes concentrating on the ground; my heart yearned for someone to see our humanity and treat us with mercy.

Chapter 14

Recognition

Before the summer is over, the fledgling storks join their parents at the feeding grounds, which are usually near wet or marshy areas.

While heading over to the dog kennels, I started thinking about how to steal food for Anna. My coat pockets would be too obvious and the first place I'd be searched if anyone became suspicious. Hardy was patiently waiting for me by the gate. When he spotted me he put his paws on the fence and wagged his tail. His behavior was a welcome distraction for the worry I carried for Anna. I couldn't help break into a smile; he looked so playful and happy to see me.

"Hi Hardy, how are you? Have you been waiting long?"

My heart melted from the kind look of recognition in his eyes. The other dogs just lay in the sun, barely even noticing I had arrived. A few of the dogs lifted their head to see who was coming in the gate, but were feeling lazy, from relaxing in the sun. Hardy immediately bounded over and began poking me with his nose to tell me, "stop and have a conversation." I rubbed his ear; the hair on it was especially soft and silky. He mouthed my coat sleeve, gently holding my arm between his teeth. He wasn't trying to bite me. He only wanted my attention in a gentle way.

"Hardy, enough!" I spoke firmly even though I didn't really need to.

He obediently released my sleeve. The fabric was threadbare and weak and one of Hardy's canine teeth tore a small hole in the fabric, exposing the lining underneath.

"Hardy, I think you just answered a prayer!"

I looked into the hole in my coat sleeve. I could probably store about a cup of food in the lining of my sleeve. I was beyond excited but I still needed to complete all of my chores and appear calm so I wouldn't arouse the guard's suspicions. I didn't want to give them any reason to suspect me. This food could mean the difference between Anna making it to the end of the war or not.

"Come on, Hardy, let's get started, shall we?"

I climbed into the first dog house. The smell of the straw reminded me of tending the nesting boxes in our hen house. I removed the day-old straw with my bare hands. This dog had a small supply of food in one corner buried under some straw. I wondered if a mouse had put the food there or if the dog had. I put several pieces through the hole in my sleeve. They fell down to the underside of my sleeve.

Hardy playfully nudged me, and I said, "Shhh, you mustn't give me away."

He sat and cocked his head sideways as if he understood my plea. He watched as I grabbed the wooden wagon and raked up the straw. He followed me from house to house as I repeated the process for every dog house in the kennel. As the weather grew warmer, many of the dogs scratched the straw out of their houses, which just made my job easier. I loved the smell of the clean, fresh straw that I pulled apart and put inside each house. Next, I emptied the metal watering tank, one bucket at a time. Thank goodness the weather was warm today. I was grateful I didn't have to do this every day! After what seemed like hours, I grabbed the stiff bristle brush and began scrubbing the green slime which had built up over the week. The warmer the weather, the faster it built up on the sides of the water trough. Hardy grabbed the small metal bucket that I had used for emptying the trough. He tilted it up as if to drain it and at the same time released it from his mouth. It landed perfectly on top of his head! He couldn't see where he was going and I had to stop cleaning the trough and pull the bucket off his head.

"Hardy, how am I going to get all of my work done, if you don't stop clowning around?"

As usual he cocked his head sideways, innocently looking at me as if to say, "Let's play."

I finally finished all of my chores and started hauling waste out to the camp dumping pit. Again I wondered what life would be like if I was able to escape. I eyed the forest. It seemed so close and yet so far and untouchable. I closed my eyes and took a deep breath. I listened for the sounds of the forest. I breathed the smell of pine needles and wood. A memory of Basil and I running down a forest path filled my mind, but it felt like lifetimes ago, not the few years it had actually been. Was I losing touch with my past, and who I had been in my life before arriving here? My eyes filled with tears and I realized I was tired, not just physically, but mentally and emotionally. I was drained. I wanted an end to this war, this camp and my captivity. For the first time I wondered if I would survive this war. I felt weak and dizzy as the ground suddenly spun up to meet my face.

I woke to someone shaking me and asking me if I was ok. It was Hardy's handler. Earlier I'd seen him from a distance.

"Yes," I answered in a daze. "What happened? I feel so tired, and my arms feel too heavy to lift."

"I think you fainted." He looked around to see if anyone was watching. "Here, let me help you up. You should try and drink some water."

Before I'd even thought about it, I'd allowed him to help me. Standing there, reeling from queasiness and fatigue, I realized a German soldier had just helped me. He could get in a lot of trouble for that act of kindness. He watched as I turned the wagon around and headed back to the kennel through the camp gate. My knees were weak and I was light headed. Still confused by the soldier's compassion, I started brushing the dogs. Perhaps later I could make sense of what had just happened.

In my weakened condition it took me more time than usual to

brush the dogs. Hardy followed me from dog to dog and sat patiently as I brushed each one. Finally, it was Hardy's turn. I spent extra time with him, because he was the last dog I groomed, and I hated to leave him. I reflected on the earlier events from the day. Maybe Hardy's handler had been in the forest, seen me faint and come to check on me. Perhaps he was just out for a walk and I hadn't noticed him. I had rarely seen him working in the camp, so only recently did I realize he was paired with Hardy. I wondered if he was the soldier who'd spoken about escaping. I hadn't seen but only heard the soldiers' quiet conversation. He seemed very kind…no wonder Hardy was so friendly.

Hardy was so much more willing to play with me than the other dogs. He really liked me. Maybe I reminded him of a girl who had cared for him as a puppy. I would never find out why he liked me so much, but I was glad he did.

Hardy was a constant reminder of Basil. They were so similar in temperament, playful yet obedient. Both followed me every-where, looked over me, and engaged me in play. I wondered if Hardy had come from Germany? What did it matter really? Maybe these comparisons, these memories, were just a cruel joke.

Look around, Ewa, look at your surroundings. I was tired of hoping and praying that my family and dog were still alive…I wanted proof, I wanted something more than hopes and dreams. My memories were starting to lose weight, they were becoming as thin as the watered down soup we ate day after day. *Please God, let me live to see my family and dog again. I know they're still alive, I can feel it. I just want to go home.* Those images were my world. They were all I arrived here with. I was afraid. My feelings were getting away from me. Hardy and Anna were taking the place of my family, diluting my memories and consuming my thoughts with concern. They were on my mind more and more every day. I felt like a traitor. I put the tools and wagon away, waited for the gate to be unlocked and headed back to the barrack following the armed soldier, like an animal weakened by exhaustion.

I was sure Anna's day of kitchen duty hadn't been as enjoyable as my day with the dogs. I'd been able to salvage about half a cup of dog food for her. I'd hidden it between the lining and outer fabric on my coat sleeve. I kept my hand in my pocket because I didn't want the dog food to come spilling out. I assumed she'd been able to steal some potato peels for herself to supplement the camp rations. I was feeling a bit stronger now as I headed through camp to our barrack. Dinner might make me feel better, even if it was only a bowl of soup; the nourishment would help. I was anxious to find out how Anna was feeling and how her day had been.

I looked up at a few clouds dotting the sky. The weather was doing its part to hurry spring along. Just as the land surrounding us was slowly changing from brown to green, Poland was slowly and steadily changing from Nazi occupation to taking back control. It wasn't as obvious as leaves forming on branches, but it was occurring. The subtle signs were there.

The fact that children were now being recruited to help in the kitchen was another indication that things were changing with the current war situation. Perhaps the usual kitchen help had been assigned to some temporary camp beautification project, or maybe sent to another war front. We'd never hear the truth from the Nazis. Honesty about their situation in the war wasn't a quality they exhibited.

Suddenly the sirens sounded – an air raid! Children began running toward their barracks for cover. There was no sound except the siren and the pounding of running feet. *Where was Anna?* Panic enveloped me. I ran into our barrack.

"Anna," I whispered loudly.

A small hand shot out from under our bunk and waved at me. Relief washed over me like water. I climbed under the bed and lay next to Anna. Shivering, she buried her face in my coat. I hugged her to my chest and whispered, "It's ok, we're ok."

She may have thought my words were for her, but they were really for me.

Chapter 15

Victory

Storks' wings are built in a way that allows them to take advantage of streams of upward moving air. Their wings are long and very wide. The black wing feathers are highlighted with a sheen of purple and green iridescence.

Victory isn't just conquering. It can also be the capacity to overcome something, or see things through to completion. I made a pact with myself that day. I would leave this place and I would take Anna and Hardy with me...*that* would be my victory. I would return home, and no matter what I found, at least I would have them by my side.

* * *

After the all-clear from the sirens and evening roll call, we lined up for our soup. It was starting to rain. I shivered and pulled my coat closer. Anna waited for me so we could eat together.

"Did you eat anything today?" I asked.

She looked around before nodding her head, *yes*. My mind flooded with relief. I knew if she was sneaking food to eat, she still had a will to live.

Anna said, "Once before the war my grandmother was baking berry pies. My cousin and I stole some of the leftover pie dough and ran outside. Our dirty hands made the buttery crust brown but we didn't care. We picked some berries and made a little pie out of the dough. We wanted to cook the pie so we built a small fire. Just as we were about to put the pie on the fire, my aunt found us and Jarek got in so much trouble, but he never let me take any of the blame. You remind me of him, Ewa. You always look out for me."

"Where is he now, Anna? Do you know?"

She closed her eyes as tears ran down her cheek. "He's gone."

I gripped her hand more firmly and realized, as day gradually changed into night, that we all had wounds that might never heal.

"Anna," I whispered, "I got some food for you today."

She smiled slightly and wiped her nose with her sleeve. As usual, her smile melted my heart and made me feel happy.

"I'll give it to you tonight when we go to bed."

"But Ewa, how will we keep the others from knowing about it?"

"I guess we'll have to wait until they fall asleep."

We made our plans and finished our soup. Most of the girls in our barrack could be trusted but we didn't want to tempt them. Hunger could make people do things they would never do if they weren't so desperate for food. I felt tempted to do things I would never have done before coming here. I would not have stolen food, told lies or planned escapes. That innocence was gone. I fully understood that I had changed. The war had taken my innocence, and turned me into someone who thought only of survival. My choices weren't based on meanness or mischievousness. I had not crossed that line; like most of the children here, I just wanted to survive long enough to go home.

Our lives followed the predictable pattern of roll call, eat, work, roll call, eat, sleep...

There were occasional changes because of new children arriving or leaving for other camps. The harshness of our lives was predictable, but it wasn't the harshness that made me emotional, it was the occasional kindness. I expected meanness out of almost everyone around me, but I didn't expect kindness, and the few times I experienced it, I cried. I'd learned early on to face my captors with a stone face. I didn't want them to see how afraid I really was. Perhaps it was that stubborn streak that my father teased me about as a child, but my stubbornness worked for me here, keeping me from showing anyone my true feelings.

Anna and Hardy were getting to me and I couldn't help myself. I found their small, but meaningful, kindnesses touched me in places I hadn't felt for so long. I felt as though I'd lost so much in life already, that I couldn't bear the thought of losing either one of them. I would do whatever it took to keep them in my life…whatever it took.

* * *

The following morning Anna and I went through our usual routine before work was assigned. I headed over to the kennel with a happy heart in anticipation of seeing Hardy. The sky was blue, yesterday's rain was gone and it was a beautiful spring day with a light breeze that smelled faintly like honeysuckle.

The potted flowers lining the central area of camp made me think about my mother's flower garden back home. Which bulbs would be popping up about now putting on their lovely spring show? She enjoyed her garden, and I loved seeing the happiness on her face as she arranged the flowers in a canning jar and placed them on our table. She said she always felt peaceful when she worked in her garden, because there was something calming about digging in the soil and tending the small green plants. The magic came from lending a hand to creation, growing something that could be useful. She had strong hands; hands that were sturdy and work calloused, hands that seemed just as comfortable working in the garden, or the kitchen while kneading bread dough. I realized how much I missed my mother. I hadn't thought about her for a while now because I'd been so concerned about Anna, the Red Cross visit and Hardy. Now, however, as I thought of her in the garden working on her flowers, I felt hopeful that she was still alive and I would be able to find her after the war. I also felt bitter that the Germans had taken her away from me for the past few years. I couldn't afford the luxury of dwelling on my bitterness, though, because it might make me distracted and I really needed to pay attention to my behavior. The Germans were very intolerant of any defiance, but submissive behavior usually kept us safe. I just kept telling myself to think about the future. *Think how good life will be when the war is over.*

When the war is over...how many times had I thought about that? It seemed to be constantly on my mind. It was an image that hung in the air like sheets on a clothesline. We were all waiting for the war to be over so we could resume our lives and take up where we left off. I felt that even some of the German soldiers were waiting for the war to end, also. They were no longer eager to conquer the world. They just wanted to return home.

Hardy brought me back to reality. As usual he was waiting by the kennel gate wagging his tail, dancing slightly and barking with delight at seeing me. I waited at the gate for someone from the barrack to come out and unlock it. I reached my hand through the gate and rubbed Hardy's head. I wanted him to calm down because drawing attention to either of us was not good.

A young man approached and quickly unlocked the gate. I walked through and stood facing Hardy.

"He likes you better than he likes me," he said, closing the gate and hooking the lock through the wire. He didn't say it in an accusatory way, just as a statement, but still I didn't turn around. I was afraid of what I would see in his eyes. "It's ok, though... I'm glad he has you."

I peeked over my shoulder at the young man. Tall, thin, blond hair, blue eyes, his characteristics represented the perfect Aryan qualities.

"Just promise me that when your release comes from this place, you'll take him with you. There shouldn't be anyone around to stop you from taking him."

I nodded my head to let him know that I would.

"I'll leave him inside the barrack so you can reach him without coming into the kennel."

I nodded my head again and quickly looked away. He didn't seem to possess the fortress of Nazi superiority that most of the guards displayed; bravado oozing out of their pores like sweat. There was a quiet kindness about him. He seemed to care about Hardy enough to arrange care for him after the war ended.

I knelt down and hugged Hardy. He bowed his head and rested it on my shoulder, his front paw on the other. He greeted me like this every day now, like he was hugging me. Basil used to hug me like that also. When I looked up again, the young soldier was gone. Stunned by his remarks, I questioned how someone's looks could be so deceiving. "Oh Hardy, you're such a goof. Come on, let's get started."

I was curious about what I'd just been told by the soldier. He must care about Hardy. He wanted him to be taken from this place and not left behind. But why wouldn't he take him? Maybe he saw how much Hardy cared for me, or perhaps he didn't want to be slowed down when he was trying to escape.

For the first time since coming here I realized that the Polish children weren't the only ones who hated being here. Maybe, just maybe, some of the young soldiers really did hate being here as well. I tried to imagine them having homes and families, but it was so difficult because they were always so stern and mean. How could it even be possible that they grew up in a loving home and yet behaved so hatefully? How did they end up here, following the orders of a mad man, making so many children suffer and live as slaves? It didn't make any sense to me. Maybe the main difference between the young guards and the children were the uniforms...some of them were slaves too; just a different kind. Victory could go so wrong when it was attained by hatred, and achieved at the expense of human life.

Chapter 16

Glory

The large wings of a stork "catch" the rising streams of air. The storks travel like gliders taking advantage of air movement. Once airborne, they don't need to flap their wings; they merely glide on the wind.

Glory happens when persistence enables us to achieve a goal despite its many obstacles. It was hard to differentiate between the subtle changes that affected our day to day routines. Perhaps, because we'd learned to accept whatever changes the Nazis threw our way, we couldn't distinguish between the changes that were life-altering and the changes that merely added to our misery. In one way we'd become like the storks I loved so much. We were mute – we had no voice.

* * *

Finally, we were three days away from the Red Cross visit. I was assigned to be a playground helper for the length of the visit. A playground had been constructed next to the school, but none of the children were allowed to play on it until the day of the inspection. Some of the children in this camp had arrived here so young that they'd never been to a playground. Would they even know how to use the giant stride swing, slide or merry-go-round?

None of the girls in our barrack were assigned to the performance. I hated the thought of missing out on the singing and special foods of the festival even if it was only pretend. I thought about what it must be like for the children to put on the show. Not only would they sing and entertain, but they would also have to put a smile on their faces and pretend they were happy little puppets, strings of coercion attached to their movements. With this realization, I was glad I hadn't been chosen to sing in the show. With my job, I didn't have to pretend I was having fun. I only had to monitor the children playing on the playground and step in if something went wrong. So there had been no rehearsals or practices for me or anyone in our barrack. Last night, after we were supposed to be asleep, we were whispering about the upcoming visit. The children involved in the performance were having to stay up later than usual to rehearse their parts, and I was relieved I hadn't been chosen, because I didn't know how I would have done it. Anna had been reassigned to the classroom for the visit, but had been severely threatened that she was to speak only if spoken to. She was not to ask any questions or do anything that would draw special attention to herself. I knew Anna took the warning seriously, and wouldn't dare cause a problem.

For the next two days we did our regular jobs until the last hour before dinner when we were instructed to report to the job assignment we'd be performing for the visit. We were rehearsing. When I arrived at the playground there were only a few children and they clearly didn't know how to use the play equipment. Eyeing the tall strider swings, confusion filled their faces like a massive flock of starlings, turning and twisting in the sky during flight.

I asked them if they wanted to swing, but they looked at me like they didn't understand, so I gently picked them up, one by one, and showed them how to hang on to the swings. Then I gently pushed them. They squealed with delight and their eyes turned into huge, wide openings of excitement as they tried to hold on with one hand and cover their mouth with the other. I could tell it was their first time and it nearly made me cry. *How did we end up in this place? How was it even possible that small children had never been to a playground and experienced the joy of swinging on a swing?* I felt so thankful that I'd had so many years at home before being sent here. I had so many great memories. I had the ability to recall, with abundant detail, many wonderful days I'd shared with my family and friends. These little ones didn't have that. I couldn't imagine surviving in this camp without my past to carry me. These youngsters had been born after the war had started. They had never known Poland before Hitler's domination, a land of nature and natural beauty, culture, traditions, and music. They had only known war, hunger and labor camps. They had come from caves in the woods, sewers in the cities and ghettos, orphanages and impoverished homes. They weren't empty inside, but had so little to draw strength from, so every day was just like the previous day. They could not remember their home and had nothing to look forward to. They had very few dreams and ideas about what their life could be like away from this regimented routine of suffering.

Maybe that was the glory... realizing what it took for a child to survive this camp, holding on persistently, despite hardships, even though there were so few memories to sustain them or help them look forward to a future. I thought about the blessings in my life. I couldn't help feeling that tightness in my chest, my eyes filling with tears. I was desperately afraid of crying, partly because if the guards saw or heard me I would receive a beating, but also I was afraid that if I started crying I would never be able to stop the flow of tears. There was a sadness in me that ran so deep I feared it was bottomless. I didn't know if I could survive knowing the depth of my grief. I pulled myself together. I had to, telling myself, "look around, take a breath, say hello to the first star of the night." Reassured, I could endure if these small children could, and I continued showing the children how to play.

* * *

The big day finally arrived. The guards woke us extra early and herded us to the showers. We were scrubbed down, rinsed off and thrown clean clothes to put on. I was grateful I'd hidden my coat in Hardy's dog house the day before. It was the one thing I still had from home, and I couldn't imagine how I'd feel if I lost it, or had it taken from me. I knew it'd be safe with Hardy. No one entered the dog houses except for the dogs and me. Thank goodness the guard hadn't noticed that I'd arrived with a coat and left without one.

After our showers we were sent to eat an early breakfast. The smell was so different from our usual food. It actually smelled like breakfast; sweet and delicious, soon my mouth was watering. We received milk, sausage and a sweet toast that reminded me of a pastry. Then we were commanded to go to the compound for our instructions.

I hardly recognized the compound. A brightly painted stage had been constructed and we were told we would be viewing the dress rehearsal. Instead of standing, we were seated on wooden benches. I couldn't help think that all of this excitement was having the exact reaction the Nazis had hoped for. The children looked surprised. You could have heard a feather floating on a breeze, it was so quiet. The seated audience of clean children eagerly anticipated the show they'd heard so much about in the past weeks. The commander came out to speak to us. Our briefing of misrepresentation and fabrication was about to commence.

An avalanche of good-will with a smile on his face, our commander began the day. It was the first time I had ever seen him smile. Usually, his speeches were like a drenching of cold, gray Nazi dogma, dragging us to the depths of our unworthiness, showing us the flaws of being Polish. I couldn't believe this was the same sour, stern-faced, man who had admonished us monthly over the last several years. Was this the same intimidating monster, who had released his fury on countless victims to make an example of them? If everything went as planned, the Nazis were actually going to pull off this huge, terrible hoax. I felt sick. I willed the disgust churning in my stomach to stay quiet. I wanted to hear the commander's message, to witness one more time, the distortion of his message of good will.

How was it possible to fool all of the delegates from the Red Cross? Would they look beyond the surface and see the skinny bodies and vacant faces? I only needed to look around for the answer, though. Hundreds of smiling, clean children wearing new clothes, new paint on the barracks, flowers, playground, school, nutritious meals – it was all part of the plan to keep their crimes hidden.

I grabbed Anna's hand, so small and cold. I looked down at my lap, willing my mind to return from the disgust at the mountain of deception I was witnessing all around me. I had to find a way to get through this day. I shook my head and vowed to myself that I would never forget the injustice of this place. I would spend the rest of my life letting the world know what Adolf Hitler and his Nazis had done to destroy the lives, hopes, and dreams of the children of Poland. Glory is the power to renounce obstacles, and complete with full consciousness, the journey before us. The storks showed us that, year after year. I had a journey to complete also.

Chapter 17

Escape

The overall population of white storks in Western Europe has declined steadily over the past century.

The Red Cross visit had come and gone. Everything had worked just as the Germans expected. That very night, after the delegates were gone and a safe distance from our camp, the old ways of doing things resumed. Clean straw mattresses were taken off our beds, and the old ones were put back on. Dinner that night was watery soup with a few potato peels. Soldiers congratulated one another on pulling off the big hoax. The camp commander had us stand at attention for over an hour and listen to another tirade about Germany's greatness.

There was a heavy, quiet grief that hung over our camp. A rug had been pulled out from under us. We lay scattered on the floor like pixie sticks…only there was no one to pick us up. For the first time in years, we had gotten to experience what life used to be like for some of us, and what life could be like for others. It lasted for what seemed like an instant and then it was gone…poof…just like a mirage. Not only was all our hard work for the last several weeks gone, but now there was nothing to look forward to.

Faced again with the cruel, oppressive austerity of camp life, I escaped to my world of memories. I thought about a trip my father and I had taken about a year before the war. We were going to drop off one of his herding dogs. We drove to a small German village in our work truck. We arrived at a farm a few miles out of a village. The farm looked very tidy and clean. When we entered the house to speak with the farmer my father realized something wasn't right. He told me to take the dog and go sit in the truck. I was very confused, but quickly did what he'd told me. I had never seen him decide to take a dog back home, but I didn't question him. The dog and I sat in the truck waiting for my father to return. I'd noticed the thin, large-eyed woman with three small children clinging to her skirts. I also remembered the sparseness of the house, but I couldn't understand what my father had seen that I hadn't. For some reason he was able to detect that his dog wouldn't be treated properly, and to this day I don't know what he saw. He only said that it wouldn't work, but he never told me why. I hoped against all odds that at least one of those Red Cross delegates had the ability to see beyond the façade; to see all of the misery and sadness that existed here with these children. Surely one of the delegates would be able to see beneath the veneer and detect the abuse?

At least one "student" escaped minutes before the Red Cross delegates arrived. It was Berta. From all the stories being told about her escape, I figured there had to be some truth in it. She was able to escape because our schedule was totally different with the Red Cross delegates here, so the sentries wouldn't expect it. Even if her escape had been detected right away it was a sure bet that an all-out manhunt wouldn't be launched. A manhunt wouldn't look good to the delegates and wouldn't fit in with the Nazis' story of an ideal school. After all, why would children want to leave if everything was so good here?

Someone thought she had hidden in a pile of fresh straw that was on the bed of a cart. When the farmer came to take back his wagon, she rode out of the camp underneath all the straw. The timing was perfect...just before the delegates' arrival. But even though there was lots of speculation, no one really knew. I was sure about one thing though; Berta was too smart and too caring to have told her plan to anyone. She knew how the girls in her barrack would suffer after the guards started questioning. If the girls knew nothing, the guards would recognize that immediately. After an escape, the rest of the children in the barrack usually paid the price of starvation or beatings until someone told what they knew. Since this escape was planned and carried out by Berta only, the guards realized quickly that no other children were involved.

I questioned in my mind if she had help from the outside. Could the Resistance have helped her or was it truly an unsuspecting farmer just doing his job? Was he a resister, who put himself and his family at great risk, or was he a collaborator with the Nazis in order avoid trouble? What would happen to the farmer who pulled the wagon out of the camp...what would happen to his family? I hoped and prayed her escape would be successful and that she would find her way back to her family. I had a feeling of great pleasure seeing the Nazis outsmarted by a young girl. I prayed that the soldiers wouldn't find her. Now like the storks, she was free to glide on the wind. If anyone could do it, Berta could. I whispered a blessing for Berta's safe passage. It gave me hope. Now I knew our turn to leave this place would come.

Chapter 18

Manifestation

Every year Poland welcomes home roughly twenty-five percent of the storks in Europe. That is why the Polish people feel every fourth stork is Polish!

Manifestation means a public demonstration, materialization, exhibition or declaration. The Nazis had shown the world the manifestation of their beliefs. A doctrine of Aryan superiority that included murder, plunder, hatred, suffering and insanity. How was it possible that anything good could come out of all that evil?

For me personally, seeing all the bad simply made me look harder for the good. It wasn't enough to see it; I wanted to search for it, feel it, touch it, connect to it – in my memories, dreams, nature, and small details of life. Some call it divine light, God's qualities, goodness or God. It didn't matter what people called it, but I knew that somewhere deep in my soul, if I could hang on to some part of goodness that still existed in the world, then the evil wouldn't win, and it wouldn't consume me like it had so many others. I suppose I owe that drive to see the good to my family. It was how they lived their life every day. An unspoken belief that divine light was always there; it was merely my job to find it, in every situation. A candle that burns day and night shows up more in the dark. I'd managed to find a few small burning candles here. The tricky part was recognizing goodness once I saw it.

* * *

Days turned into weeks and weeks turned into months. Four full months passed since the delegates visited our camp. The size of our camp was steadily diminishing as children were shipped to other camps. I felt like the Germans were working at a frenzied pace...but maybe I was so tired it just seemed that way. Some days felt like I was walking through syrup. The heaviness of my arms and legs were weighed down by a force I could not explain.

Memories continued to sustain me and got me thinking about how much I missed school. The thought of reading a book again, or sitting in a warm classroom and learning something new, was exhilarating. I longed to pick an apple from the tree I passed every day on my way to school. Not just any apple – a paper apple, with ivory skin and flesh. They dotted the tree on the road from our farm to school. So juicy, the memory made my mouth water. I would eat at least two every day. Basil loved them as well.

I wondered what had happened to the rest of my school mates, children I had known for my entire life. Had they ended up in similar camps? There was only one child from my town in this camp, but I hadn't had an opportunity to speak with her.

A new girl named, Kashia, told us how her whole village had escaped by abandoning their homes and farms and running into the woods. She told us how they'd dug caves, chopped small trees and used the logs to reinforce the walls. She said it was dirty and cold and it seemed like you were always wet. Kashia spoke about the barbed wire fence being the only difference between this camp and her cave. She said it was hard to be quiet and hungry and cold all the time. The children weren't allowed to play for fear of being heard by German patrols. Fires were only allowed on days when the weather was so bad that smoke couldn't be detected. I felt like Kashia might be able to show Anna and me how to survive once we got out of here. Like I used to, she knew which plants to eat and which ones were poisonous. She seemed to know things that living in the woods for years will teach you....like using caution when something doesn't look quite right, knowing which stars to use for directions, choosing water that is safe to drink, and building a small shelter. I didn't trust that I would remember everything I used to know about the forest. When our freedom came, I hoped I could convince Kashia to travel with us for a few days at least.

Some of the children had come here from orphanages. They spoke of similarly overcrowded, miserable conditions before coming here, but there wasn't barbed wire, soldiers on patrol, or factory work. That always took time to adjust to.

In our camp, several conditions remained constant: work, hunger, exhaustion and fear. My work in the kennel wasn't as exhausting as it had been. I was actually getting stronger from sneaking small bits of dog food every day. My stomach wasn't as empty as it had been when I started working in the kennels. Anna had been assigned to the kitchen for one week now, so the potato peels she was sneaking were making a difference. At last our hunger didn't wake us up at night, like it used to. I was feeling slightly hopeful today. *Maybe we would be out of this place soon.* So many "maybes." Life teetered on the possibilities; like walking through a maze blindfolded, I felt my way, unsure of where I would end up.

Several months had passed since the soldier had spoken to me about taking Hardy. I considered what that conversation might mean as I started my work in the kennel. Hardy wasn't around today and I missed him terribly. *He must be out on patrol.* I cleaned the kennel, hauled fresh water, brushed the few dogs that were there and started hauling the waste to the pit just outside the camp. It was always a bit scary being outside the camp fence, as I worried that a soldier would think I was trying to escape and shoot me. I kept a slow, deliberate pace and hummed a song I'd learned in school so my behavior wouldn't be seen as threatening in any way. I pulled the wagon to the edge of the pit and began shoveling out the waste. There was the forest, just a few yards away, as beautiful as ever, begging me to take a short walk and forget about all I'd been forced to endure over the last few years. Leaves changing color, squirrels stocking up for winter, cones falling in preparation for renewal and new growth to begin again in the spring, life still resided there.

I looked up at the guard tower. Guns ready, helmets in place, stance of control and authority; the Nazis were ready to defend their territory, and all of the children that now belonged to them. I didn't think they really cared about the land or children they were patrolling. I was at a dead-end. Would I be able to find a way out of here? The Ghetto we were housed in was being liqui-dated and we could hear the sounds of terror and grief as families were ripped apart and lives were hurled to destruction. I could hear the storks out on their nests, occasionally clattering their bills; it sounded a bit like distant machine gun fire. It was their way of greeting one another. It was reassuring and yet a bit unset-tling how nature went on with its natural rhythm and flow when all of mankind and the world seemed to be acting so crazy and chaotic. They would be leaving any day now for their winter feeding grounds in Africa, and I couldn't help but wonder if I would survive another winter in captivity and be alive to see them upon their return in the spring.

Winter would be coming soon, and I'd naïvely planned on the war being over by now. Disappointment weighed me down as if I was hauling a backpack full of rocks. My legs felt heavy; my heart was beating slowly from the effort to keep going despite my miscalculation.

"Look for the light, Ewa," Grandfather whispered in my ear.

My heart lightened. "I will, grandpa."

I turned the wagon around and headed back through the gate.

Chapter 19

Liberation

The legend that the European White Stork brings babies is believed to have originated in northern Germany, perhaps because storks arrive on their breeding grounds nine months after midsummer.

Connection is a link or a bond. Joining or relating two or more things. I'd made connections with Anna and Hardy. I would not be able to leave without them. They, along with my memories and my love of nature had kept me alive. I didn't know how we'd get out of here, but I was sure about one thing.... I'd take the opportunity when it came.

Another winter. *Please God, may it be my last in this misery.* It had always been vital to do everything within my power to stay alive, but now it was even more crucial. The youngest children were being transported out, and only the children ten and older were allowed to stay and work. Anna had been reassigned to a munitions factory. I was still attending the dogs and cleaning the kennels, even though their numbers were dwindling as well. Slowly and methodically, I loaded and transported all the waste out to the dumping pit. I turned and looked back at the camp, a picture forever imprinted on my brain and my soul. Through the rows of wire I saw the buildings. Again, the color brown stood out. Rows of brown desolation, vacant buildings of hunger and deprivation. Even the buildings looked starved. I eyed the lookout sentry in his tower. He stood fixed, gazing at the camp and fields with binoculars, oblivious to the suffering around him. I wondered how it was possible for him to not see it.

Usually I saw the soldiers on sentry duty with their guns ready. Today, however, there were very few patrolling the camp, and they didn't look like they were watching the inmates. I noticed they were looking up at the sky. Even though it was cold, the sun was shining, but it looked as if it was snowing. White pieces of paper were floating down from the sky. I saw one of the sentries reach out and grab one. A piece floated down out of the sky and landed in the wagon. I looked around to see if the soldiers in the guard tower were looking at me, but they were looking up at all the white falling from the sky.

In three different languages, the paper said the war was over! I quickly folded the paper and put it in the bottom of my shoe. I could hardly wait to show the others in my block. *Could it be true?* It didn't look like the war was over. I finished emptying the wagon and headed back to the kennel. Walking back I saw soldiers in small groups, talking quietly among themselves. There seemed to be an uneasy restlessness hanging over the camp. I checked the kennel one more time for Hardy, but he still wasn't back.

After putting the wagon and tools away I headed out of the maze of fences and gates toward the barracks. I entered our building and found everyone sitting on their bunks, including Anna. They were wrapped in rags, huddled together for warmth. I thought about the years we'd spent here, the struggles we'd fought through, the deprivation we'd endured. I looked at their thin faces, shaved heads, bruise-covered skin. All bore testament to the years of slave labor we'd survived.

We survived, WE SURVIVED...those words hit me like a wall of water, and my stomach fluttered. I grabbed the post to steady myself. I climbed silently onto our bunk. Was this truly the end of the war? I couldn't believe it! Why so quiet? No roll call, no dinner, no sound, nothing... I wanted to show Anna the paper I'd found but was too afraid of causing a commotion if anyone else saw it.

After a while under the protection of darkness, Kashia crouched low, crawled over and peeked out the window. The lights that normally scanned the camp were black. Was this blackout an attempt by our captors to hide the camp? Were we going to be bombed by the allies like the Germans had done to us at the start of the war? We all wondered about the total darkness, and the complete lack of noise....could it actually be true? Had the German soldiers abandoned the camp? Somewhere in the distance we could hear the low rumble of tanks, transport trucks and planes.

Kashia thought that she could see the camp gates open, but it was too dark to tell for sure. None of us wanted to risk getting shot so close to liberation. Perhaps it was a trick. Morning light would show us the truth for sure. I made the girls promise to be absolutely silent, then pulling the paper I'd found out of my shoe, I read it to them. The black print told about the war being over. They all stared at the ground as I showed them the notice. Then three other girls pulled the same papers out of their shoes. Some had tears rolling down their dirt streaked faces forming a clean trail down their cheeks. It seemed like it was too good to be true. Many had lost hope long ago and were just barely surviving hour by hour. Others had been here so long that this was the only home they could remember. Some of us had vivid memories and were eager to leave but also a little hesitant of what we might find upon returning to our homes. No matter what I might find upon my return home, I knew it couldn't possibly be as horrific as this camp.

A light rain began to fall, with clouds covered the moon and the stars, and a heavy darkness covered the camp as we closed our eyes on our last night in this barren room that had been our prison. I had Anna by my side. I'd look for Hardy first thing in the morning. I pulled the filthy rag we'd been using for a blanket over us. I said a quick silent prayer, thankful that liberation was finally, really here. I'd gone over and over this moment many times in my mind, but somehow now that it was possibly here, it didn't match the pictures in my mind. I guess I didn't think about having to get myself back home. I let my worries, confusion and excitement be engulfed in the blackness of the night; for now I just needed sleep.

We woke at first light. There were still no camp sounds, no lookouts in the tower, no soldiers around. Occasionally, we could hear dogs barking in the distance. One of the older children walked into our barrack and warned us that Russian soldiers were closing in, and that we should leave the camp as quickly as possible. The rain had stopped falling and the sun was just rising. We got up and looked at one another.

We saw other children walking quietly by our window – it was really true… we were free! We had made it! We'd survived the war! I had imagined my freedom numerous times over the long years of internment but never like this. We weren't acting like children, happy and excited. We grabbed our few belongings and headed out the door. Quickly and silently the camp was emptying out. Most of us had only one plan; find some food then head for home. We couldn't quite believe we were actually free, and after years of forced quiet and forbidden speech, I don't think we knew what to say.

Anna grabbed my hand as we headed out the door.

"Anna, I have to go find Hardy! Come with me," I said.

"Ewa, how will we ever take care of him? We have no food."

"I know, but I'll think of something…please, Anna."

Anna was clearly uneasy but willing to give me a few more minutes to find Hardy. "Ok, but I'm going to go search the kitchen. I think I might know where to find some potatoes or beets, and maybe there is still some bread."

I walked over quickly to the kennels, while Anna headed to the kitchen. I didn't want to waste any time in case the Germans came back, or the Russians showed up. The kennels were empty! Now what?

I waited for Anna to return from her search in the kitchen. When Anna saw me without Hardy she offered a thought:

"Maybe they took the dogs with them."

"But I heard barking this morning, Anna, just a short while ago."

We listened to see if we could hear the barking again, but there was nothing.

"We'd better go," I said. Sadly, I turned around and headed for the main gate. Then I remembered the soldier who'd spoken to me about taking Hardy. "Anna, I just remembered something. Give me one more minute, then we'll leave, I promise."

Anna nodded, shifting her weight from foot to foot to keep warm.

Hopefully, he was in the soldiers' barracks.

"Wait here, Anna."

I walked back to the barracks that housed the dog handlers. I quietly opened the door.

"Hardy," I called.

I heard a bark, then some whining, followed by more barking. I was too terrified to step inside so I called his name again. Suddenly, a wooden table started sliding toward me with Hardy hooked to it by a rope! One of the table legs caught the corner edge of the wall and broke apart with a loud cracking sound, sending splinters of wood flying everywhere. Hardy reached me with only one table leg still attached to the rope. Tail wagging, he immediately started licking my face; I was trying to untangle the rope from the table leg but Hardy's excitement was making it hard.

"Hardy, sit!"

He obediently sat, head cocked sideways, trying to remain patient while I untangled the mess. I grabbed the rope and headed back to Anna.

"Ewa, you found him!" Anna grabbed my free hand and with Hardy on one side and Anna on the other we walked through the gate that had stood in the way of a life I longed to leave behind, and toward a life I longed to regain.

I took my first breath of freedom and looked up, searching the bright blue sky for a stork. It was winter, and the storks were long gone and months away from returning. But my heart was full of hope and longing for home. My eyes filled with tears as Anna dropped my hand and pointed in amazement at a stork flying quietly overhead, its large, black-tipped wings making the soft swishing sound I knew so well. I smiled as my grandfather's face slid into memory, a blessing and a measure of good luck was upon our heads now. "Thank you, Grandpa."

I can't say why the stork was there at that time of year. Perhaps it had been injured and too weak to fly when the others had migrated south. Maybe it was smaller than the others and too young to fly. I didn't know, but I felt grateful for the opportunity to see it. Connection is also made by the beliefs and memories that bind you to another, no matter how many miles separate you. Knowledge of life's source is the realization of all the abundance that exists on earth. My time here had shown me that nature and all of creation continued to move through life cycles and generate new life, no matter what humans were doing. Poland was overflowing with potential, abundance and life. I'd been searching for God's goodness and somehow I'd managed to find and hang on to some of the light that still existed in the world. Maybe it was possible to see the light amidst all this darkness. Maybe it was a gift from God providing me with a spark to light my way. After all, my name is Ewa, and it means "life".

Grandpa's saying came out of my mouth. "If God came down from heaven, he'd come to Poland because it would remind him of the Garden of Eden."

Anna squeezed my hand.

* * *

Sovereignty is authority, dominance, or the final gathering of all resources. From 1921 to April of 1945 Adolf Hitler attempted world dominance. His programs for racial purification, social cleansing, Germanization, and developing a "Master Race" all played a part in the destruction of millions of lives. It is estimated that six million Polish citizens lost their lives during Hitler's reign.

Glossary

Allies – Nations that support one another in their war effort. Germany and Russia supported one another at the start of WWII.

Aryan – In Nazi Doctrine, a non-Jewish Caucasian of Nordic stock. Adolf Hitler believed that the Aryan race was an ideal, pure, superior race and that this entitled them to expand their lands by taking what they wanted.

Blackout – Turn out or conceal all lights that might be visible to enemy air raids.

Colonization – To enter another country and settle the land there, usually displacing the people who already live there.

Concentration camp – a place of confinement, a prison.

Depolonization – to destroy; in this story it meant to destroy the Polish people, including their language, culture, traditions, beliefs and country.

Deportation - To expel from a place or country. In this case the Polish people were deported from their homes and forced to live and work in concentration camps and labor camps.

Emaciation – to lose too much weight. Many of the concentration camp prisoners weren't fed enough to keep weight on their bodies.

Ewa – Polish spelling for Eva. Her name means "life."

Feast of the Annunciation - March 25, is one of the most important holy days in the Catholic Church calendar. It celebrates the actual Incarnation of Jesus in the womb of His mother, Mary.

Germanization – to make or become German in character, thought, language etc.

Ghetto – any section of a city where many members of a certain racial or ethnic group live or are restricted from leaving.

Goose step- A marching step where the legs swing high and straight out.

Hitler, Adolf –Leader of the Nazi Party. He was chancellor of Germany from 1933-1945. He was a dictator and center of Nazi Germany. His goal was to establish a "New Order" of absolute Nazi German. He transformed the Weimar Republic into the Third Reich, a single-party dictatorship based on the totalitarian and autocratic ideology of Nazism.

Inmates – a person confined with others in an institution or prison.

Lent – in the Christian religion an annual season of fasting and penitence in preparation for Easter.

Nazi - a member of the National Socialist German Workers' party of Germany. In 1933 under Adolf Hitler, the Nazi party seized political control of the country, suppressing all opposition and establishing a dictatorship over all cultural, economic, and political activities of the people, and promoted belief in the supremacy of Adolf Hitler as Führer. The party was officially abolished in 1945 at the conclusion of World War II.

Rehabilitate - to restore to a condition of good health, ability to work, or the like.

Resettlement - the act or instance of settling or being settled in another place. The Nazis used this phrase to refer to forced deportation. Millions of people were resettled into ghettos, concentration camps and labor camps.

Resistance – During WWII the resistance was anyone or any group of people involved in undermining and opposing the efforts of the Nazis and those governments who supported the Nazis.

The Führer- A German word (führen) for the term leader. Adolf Hitler was Germany's absolute dictator during WWII.

Transport trains – trains that were used in WWII to take people from their homes to concentration camps. The trains were very full and the people riding them had no bathrooms, food, water, or place to sit or rest. Many people died during the transports since it would take several days for them to travel to the camps.

The White Storks of Poland

White storks have been coming to Poland for hundreds of years. Poland has over 52,000 pairs of storks that come to breed and nest. The storks form colonies while breeding and several pairs will nest near one another. Storks don't mind nesting close to each other, and are not bothered by their stork neighbors. Storks form monogamous pairs for the entire length of the breeding season.

They do not migrate or overwinter together but some pairs have paired up again in successive years because of their strong attachment to their nesting site. The males are the ones who usually arrive to the nest site first. It is the male's job to prepare the nest for the female. A male will greet the arriving female with a head-shaking, crouching display. If the male accepts the female as his mate, they will show they are bonded by an up-down display. When they perform this display, they hold their wings out away from their sides while pumping their heads up and down. This is usually accompanied by bill-clattering. If the birds perform a shorter courtship display it usually means they have been paired in previous years.

Their nests are huge, around six feet by ten feet. They are built of branches and sticks, and lined with twigs, grass, paper, rags, and leaves. They are often six to nine feet deep. The nests are reused year after year, but the breeding pair will add to the structure of the nest each season. They are particularly fond of building their nests on man-made structures like roofs, chimneys, towers, telephone poles, and haystacks. Nests can also be found in trees, cliff ledges and even on the ground.

The female usually lays three to five eggs, and the pair take turns constantly sitting on the egg. After thirty-three to thirty-four days of incubation, they hatch covered with white down and black bills. Both parents feed the chicks for about nine weeks until they fledge. The young birds will not reach maturity until they are four years old. The storks can live and breed successfully for more than thirty years.

The Polish people are very fond of their storks, and have viewed them as a symbol of prosperity and good luck for hundreds of years. A Polish folk tale tells how frogs, lizards, snails and other pests were multiplying excessively, and became so numerous that they caused great problems. God gathered them all in a sack and told a man to empty the sack into the sea. Curiosity got the best of the poor human and he opened the sack! All escaped, so God changed the man into a stork to hunt them and gather them up.

No other European country can boast about as many nesting pairs of storks as Poland. They are the national symbol of Poland. Storks, being constantly present in Polish landscape, remain its vivid symbol and have found their place in their folktales, proverbial sayings, superstitions, church holidays and culture. For those reasons the stork is an inseparable symbol.

The history behind the story

There are numerous accounts of how the Holocaust affected the Jewish community. There are very few accounts of how other groups of people – Poles, Slavs, and Gypsies, to name some, were also the target of Nazi policies of racial purity and genocide. The following two books were extremely helpful in writing this story.

Did The Children Cry? Hitler's War against Jewish and Polish Children, 1939-45 by Richard C. Lukas (Hippocrene Books, Inc., 1994). Lucas concentrates on outlining the specific ways the Nazis established the most efficient killing factory in history and the history of genocide of Polish children. This book is based on eye-witness accounts, interviews, and research.

Forgotten Holocaust: The Poles under German Occupation 1939-1944 by Richard C. Lukas (Hippocrene Books, Inc., 1990). This book chronicles, with thorough documentation, Germany's occupation and destruction of Poland's culture and people.

In addition, some of the history behind the story was found online at these two sources:

The Jewish Virtual Library – an article titled "Stolen Children" by Gitta Sereny.

The Museum of Tolerance Online – an article titled "Non-Jewish Children in the Camps" by Sybil Milton.

Approximately 200,000 Polish children were taken from their homes between 1939 and 1945. Under the Nazi occupation, Poland was taken over, occupied and settled by German settlers causing forced resettlement of the original inhabitants. Poland was racially and geographically consolidated into Germany.

Eventually all Polish children between the ages of two and twelve were examined and segregated into two categories: "racially valuable or worthless," as Himmler once wrote. Children found to be racially worthless were either sent home or, if old enough and capable, sent to Germany to work. Those with racial potential were taken to one of three centers in the Warthegau, where further tests were conducted.

Forgotten Holocaust, on page 25, cites Himmler: "I would consider it right if small children of Polish families who show especially good racial characteristics were apprehended and educated by us in special institutions and children's homes which must not be too large."

In December 1942, a camp for Polish children and youth known as Litzmannstadt was established in a separate area within the walls of the Lodz ghetto. The main gate to the camp was located on Przemyslowa Street; which is why it was often referred to as "The Camp on Przemyslowa Street."

On November 28, 1942, the Main Security Office of the Reich explained that it would be a camp for adolescent Poles, those adolescents deemed to be criminals or uncared-for, "who, therefore, are a dangerous element both for the German children, and because of the fact that they could continue their criminal activity."

The camp was made to look like an educational facility to rehabilitate juvenile offenders. In reality though, it was a concentration camp for children and youth up to the age of 16. The young inmates had numbers instead of names, wore gray prison clothes and clogs, and worked from morning to night. They were also subjected to routine beatings. The camp area was surrounded by a high fence made up of planks and patrolled by German sentries.

The camp prisoners primarily came from the areas incorporated into the Reich once they had conquered Poland. Some children were taken from orphanages; some were taken from parents who'd been arrested for their involvement in the resistance movement. Some were children who had been taken from their families for "Germinization" but had been unable to pass the exhaustive racial examinations.

By January 1945, an estimated 1,600 Polish children went

through this camp. The exact number of inmates is difficult to establish because many of the records are missing. When the war was over, there were about 900 prisoners in the camp.

The children worked just as their peers did in the ghetto, on the other side of a high wall. The children stitched clothes, made straw shoes, mended knapsacks and straightened out needles. Many of them died of starvation, cold and emaciation, especially during the typhus epidemic that broke out in late 1942 and early 1943. Records document 136 deaths.

The Polish children in this camp were completely isolated from the outside world and had no contact with the people from the other side of the wall. A branch of this camp also operated on a private estate in Dzierzana, 15 kilometers from Lodz.

Today, only the old camp administrative building at 34 Przemyslowa St. remains. For many years after the war, people did not know about this camp for Polish children and youth. In May 1971, the Broken Heart Monument was unveiled in Szarych Szeregow Park, a somber reminder of the young victims. The monument, designed by Jadwiga Janus and Ludwik Mackiewicz, is located just outside the old camp area. The inscription reads, *"They've taken your lives. Today we can offer you only memory."*

To that inscription I would add one thing: "Love leaves a memory no one can steal."

**TOP HAT
BOOKS**

Historical fiction that lives.

We publish fiction that captures the contrasts, the achievements, the optimism and the radicalism of ordinary and extraordinary times across the world.

We're open to all time periods and we strive to go beyond the narrow, foggy slums of Victorian London. Where are the tales of the people of fifteenth century Australasia? The stories of eighth century India? The voices from Africa, Arabia, cities and forests, deserts and towns? Our books thrill, excite, delight and inspire.

The genres will be broad but clear. Whether we're publishing romance, thrillers, crime, or something else entirely, the unifying themes are timescale and enthusiasm. These books will be a celebration of the chaotic power of the human spirit in difficult times. The reader, when they finish, will snap the book closed with a satisfied smile.